MURDER ON WINTER ISLAND
A KARA HILDER MYSTERY

JENNA ST. JAMES

Murder on Winter Island

Jenna St. James

Copyright © 2023 by Jenna St. James.

Published by Jenna St. James

All Rights Reserved. No part of this publication may be reproduced without the written permission of the author.

This is a work of fiction. Names and characters are either the product of the author's imagination or are used fictitiously, and any resemblance to actual persons, living or dead, business establishments, events, or locales is entirely coincidental.

❋ Created with Vellum

I

"I can't get over how well they play together," Bettina Davers said as she popped a grape into her mouth. "They look like they're having a ball."

I glanced over at my scowling tuxedo cat, Savage, and barely suppressed a smiled. I could have told her the truth—that Savage was miserable and was probably plotting all our deaths—but I kept that secret to myself. After all, I was the only one in the bookstore able to hear Savage speak. Well, except for Link, the sword-wielding pixie who lived in my tree stump and helped me solve crimes…but he was too busy enjoying Savage's misery to pay any attention to Bettina.

Zahara nodded. "You should definitely come visit more during lunch and bring Savage."

Bettina and Zahara Davers were twin witches who owned the magical bookstore, Double Trouble, in Mystic Cove…the town where I now lived. They'd also just adopted three playful kittens, Snowflake, Midnight, and Midge. When the twins called earlier and begged me to stop by for lunch and some playtime with Savage, I couldn't say no.

Savage had said no, of course. But in the end, I ignored his objections, strapped his cat helmet onto his head, and drove my Ducati to the bookstore. Link had also hitched a ride in the saddlebag.

I glanced at my watch. "Your thirty minutes is almost up. You'll have to open your bookstore soon."

Bettina groaned and ran her hand through her blue and black hair. "It always goes by so quickly."

The twins closed the shop for thirty minutes every day so they could enjoy a peaceful, quiet lunch. The bookstore could get pretty rowdy at times…what with all the extra characters who came to life inside the store. There was Gollum, Casper, and even a fire-breathing dragon who swooped down from the rafters and scared me every time I stepped inside the store. Granted, the fire wasn't real, but it was still scary. The whole supernatural thing was still relatively new to me, after all.

I'd only learned about the paranormal world back in January. That was when Zane—a fallen angel who was now my crime-solving partner and celestial boyfriend—had turned up at a dive-bar in Seattle and snatched me away on my fortieth birthday. He'd flown me to Mystic Cove to meet Rota, my long-lost Valkyrie grandmother.

It was then I discovered not only was I a Valkyrie like Rota, but I could also wield magic thanks to my dad, Callum Bram. Callum was a bird shifter and powerful witch. I'd also had no idea Callum existed until recently. My mother—Rota's daughter—had fled Mystic Cove for the human world when she discovered she was pregnant, and then was murdered before anyone back in Mystic Cove could learn about me.

I was brought up by an elderly Sensei who died when I was

just twenty. I'd spent the next twenty years believing I was completely alone in the world. But all that had changed just six months ago.

"How long will Zane be gone this time?" Zahara asked.

I bent down and scratched Snowball under the chin... ignoring Savage's huff. "A few days. He's supposed to be back Saturday or Sunday. Just depends on how the apprehension goes."

Bettina grinned. "Seeing as how it's only Thursday, what're you gonna do for three days without him?"

I rolled my eyes. "I'm sure I'll get along just fine. I have Savage and Link to keep me company."

Savage hissed at me. *"I'm not speaking to you for at least a week."*

I stuffed a baked jalapeño chip in my mouth so I wouldn't laugh out loud.

"What did he say?" Bettina asked.

"He said he'd be glad to keep me company while Zane's away," I lied.

The first time I'd heard Savage talk, I'd nearly fainted. Communicating with animals was a trait I'd inherited from my father. I couldn't shift into a bird like him—at least, not that I knew of—but I *could* hear animals speak.

"I don't think that's what he said," Bettina said.

Zahara raised both hands in the air excitedly. "We should all get together for a girls' weekend Saturday. You, me, Bettina, and Crystal. It'll be fun."

Crystal Nobel was a winged-horse shifter I'd recently met during a murder investigation. We'd quickly become friends. Rota said it was destined to be because at one time, Valkyries rode the skies on their winged horses collecting the fallen and delivering them to Valhalla. I wasn't sure about all that. What I knew to be true was the instant connection and friendship I had with Crystal.

"Sure," I said. "We can meet at my cottage and—"

"Outta me way, lasses!" Link cried in his Scottish brogue as he swooped down from the rafters atop the back of the magical fire-breathing dragon. "I'm after me some furry kittens!"

At this, the three kittens mewed in glee and jumped in the air as high as their tiny legs would allow.

"Not if we get you first!"

"Come back here you scared Pixie!"

"We'll eat you for dinner!"

Savage picked up an emery board off the counter and started to file his nails. *"Someone's getting gutted. If it's a pixie, then so be it!"*

This time, I did laugh. "Savage Beast! You put that nail filer down this minute! You aren't gutting anyone."

Bettina and Zahara laughed so hard, tears filled their eyes.

"You poor girl," Zahara said as she stood and stretched. "Do you think Savage and Link will ever get along?"

"I'm hopeful," I said.

"Never!" Savage exclaimed.

"Never!" Link echoed from somewhere overhead.

The kittens were making an awful racket as they tried to jump up onto the bookshelves and catch Link.

"I bet you wish now you'd gone with Zane," Bettina said.

I shook my head and threw away my empty bag of chips in the trash can under the counter. "No way. He was flying to some remote location in Russia. Like in the Arctic Circle or something."

"PADA really needs to hire more detectives," Bettina said.

I worked for PADA, the Paranormal Apprehension and Detention Agency—a government agency who had the last word on all things paranormal as far as criminal matters went. Unfortunately, PADA detectives were spread too thin. The global supernatural world was a large place, and there were not enough agents to go around. Not only did Zane and I help the police in Mystic Cove whenever a murder happened, but we also had to travel and work when there weren't any local paranormal police available. Those were fun assignments because we usually went undercover. Other times, like now, Zane had to travel to remote locations to apprehend and deliver criminals to PADA's prison.

"Zane told me PADA was thinking of adding a Remote Location team," I said. "Which would be great. Less away time for us."

"It's twelve-thirty," Zahara said. "I guess I'll go flip the sign to open."

My cell phone rang, and I snatched it off the counter. Smiling when I saw it was my grandmother, I put her on speakerphone. "Hey, Rota. How's our new interim mayor today?"

A couple weeks ago, the long-time mayor of Mystic Cove had been arrested and sent to a PADA prison for life. That left the town with a vacancy that needed to be filled. Rota had stepped up and assumed responsibility until an election could be held.

"Doing mayoral crap," she said. "You alone?"

"Sort of. I'm with Bettina and Zahara."

"That's it?" Rota demanded.

Zahara quickly flipped the sign on the front door back to closed.

"That's it," I said. "What's going on?"

"There's been a murder out on Winter Island," Rota said. "Sheriff called me to let me know. He said he called PADA, and they informed him Zane was away for a couple days, but you were available and able to take the case."

Link floated down to the counter and landed next to my hand. "I can help as well, Rota."

"Won't you freeze?" I asked. "I mean, won't your wings get cold?"

"Aye," Link said. "But ye are a Valkyrie and a witch, lass."

I laughed. "Okay. What does that mean?"

"I know the twins have taught you how to conjure a flame," Link said, dropping his accent. "You can keep me warm. Plus, I'm sure either you or the twins can outfit me with something warm to wear."

"We can do that," Zahara said.

"Who was killed?" Bettina asked.

"Tentative ID is Mya Harlan," Rota said. "But Doc Treestone will need to make the pronouncement. He's on his way to the ferry now. Sheriff Stiles said he'd escort you and Doc Treestone over to the island. He should be at the ferry in ten minutes. Can you get there by then?"

I smiled. "Seeing as how the ferry is at the end of the street here on the boardwalk not twenty yards away…I'm sure I can make it."

"Will you come home tonight or stay there?" Rota asked.

A twinge of excitement ran through me. I hadn't thought about staying on the island overnight, but now that Rota had said it, I totally wanted to. "I'd love to stay on Winter Island, but I don't have anything with me."

"We can give you clothes," Bettina said.

"And any toiletries you might need," Zahara added.

"Then it's settled," I said. "I think I'll stay on the island to investigate."

"I figured you'd say that. There's a B&B in town called Snow Haven where you can stay," Rota said. "I've already called ahead and booked you a room. Side note—the victim worked part time at Snow Haven. I only know this because when I called, the owner answered the phone, and she was crying. When I asked if she was okay, she told me her part-time employee had just been killed. I'm assuming we're talking about the same woman. Not that many people on the island."

"About how many people are there?" I asked. "Do you know?"

"Just under a thousand on the entire island," Rota said.

"Did you know this Mya Harlan?" I asked.

"Nope," Rota said. "Can't say that I did."

I looked at the twins, but they both shook their heads.

"Thanks, Rota. I'll call you tonight with an update," I said.

I disconnected and slipped my phone in my pocket. "Do you also have a phone charger I can use?"

"Give me five minutes to throw everything in a bag for you," Zahara called as she sprinted to the back of the bookstore and up the stairs leading to their apartment overhead.

"I'm not going," Savage said.

I rolled my eyes. "You *are* going. I don't have time to run you back to the cottage."

"He can stay here with us," Bettina volunteered.

"Yes! Stay here!"

"We can play all day and night!"

"You can give us rides on your back, Uncle Savage!"

The three kittens tripped over themselves trying to get to Savage.

"On second thought," Savage said, *"a trip to a remote winter island sounds positively wonderful."*

I let out a bark of laughter. "I think Savage will go with Link and me."

"If you're sure," Bettina said. "He's more than welcome to stay."

"I'm sure," I said. "But thanks for the offer."

It wasn't long before footsteps thudded on the back stairs, and Zahara slid into the front of the bookstore carrying a medium-sized carpetbag. "You have two sets of clothes, thermals, pajamas, and I stuffed in gloves, a down jacket, and snow boots for when you reach the island. Those jeans should be fine for right now, but not the shoes."

I glanced down at my tennis shoes. "I didn't think about winter apparel. It's eighty-two today, and the sun is shining."

"And just thirty minutes away," Bettina said, "it snows every day."

"Oh, joy," Savage grumbled.

"Thanks, Zahara." I grabbed the bag from her. "I'll return all this when I get back."

"Here." She held out a miniature pink and yellow puffy winter jacket to Link. "I know it's not ideal, but it's all I had."

I laughed. "Where did you find that?"

Zahara grinned. "My Barbie collection from when I was a little girl."

Link slid his arms into the jacket and pulled it tight. "I like it."

"Let me cut some slits for your wings," Zahara said, pulling out scissors from under the counter.

Link turned his back to her and stood still while Zahara cut two small slits into the fabric. Seconds later, his wings popped out, and he shot into the air, pink pixie dust leaking from one wing.

"I love it!" he said. "Thank ye, lass. 'Tis a true treasure."

"I suppose I'm just supposed to freeze to death?" Savage lamented.

I laughed. "I doubt you'll freeze to death. You have fur."

"Does Savage need a coat?" Bettina asked. "We can conjure a cat suit for him."

Zahara nodded. "Maybe one to match Link's jacket?"

Savage's entire body shuddered, and he shook his head emphatically. *"No. Do not put me in some fluffy pink monstrosity."*

"I think he'll be fine," I said. "Right, Savage?"

Instead of answering, Savage turned and flicked his tail at me as he strolled toward the front door.

"Guess that means we're ready to go. Do you guys mind if I park my Ducati in your alley?"

"Of course not," Zahara said.

"Don't forget my helmet," Link said. "Just in case."

"You can forget mine, if you like."

I hugged each of the twins. "See you in a couple days."

2

"Is this your first trip to Winter Island?" Doc Treestone asked as he helped me onto the pirate ship.

Doc Treestone, polar bear shifter and the town's medical examiner, was a large man who stood well over six feet and had a wide chest and broad shoulders. Today, his long, salt and pepper hair was pulled back into a low ponytail.

"It is," I said, dropping my carpetbag onto a vacant bench seat. "I wish it were under better circumstances." I glanced around the ship and smiled. "This is spectacular."

The ferry that took travelers back and forth from Mystic Cove to Winter Island was actually an old pirate ship. At night, the masts would glow so brightly, I could see them from the lighthouse next to my cottage.

Link hovered near my shoulder. "Ahoy, Matey! Nothin' like a rough sea ride to get yer sea legs under ye."

"The boat is made of teakwood," Doc Treestone said. "Nice and sturdy for the ride over. Don't let Link fool you."

Link chuckled. "Just pullin' yer sea leg, lass."

I glanced up to where the captain stood high above me, looking out over the ship. He was dressed in a full period captain's costume, which looked remarkably accurate. When he caught me staring, he winked, and his body flickered.

"What?" I whispered.

Doc Treestone chuckled. "Captain Ron actually died over three hundred years ago, but he still captains his boat."

"I bet he and Mosley have a lot to talk about," Savage said as he curled up on top of the carpetbag.

Mosley was a two-hundred-year-old ghost who guarded the lighthouse next to my cottage. When he wasn't busy overlooking the ocean, he sometimes sat in the graveyard next to the lighthouse.

Sheriff Stiles strode across the plank and stopped next to us. "They only take the ferry across a couple times during the day, but when I explained the circumstances, Captain Ron and his crew were happy to help."

I glanced over at the man lifting the drawbridge. "Is he a ghost too?"

"The entire crew is," Sheriff Stiles said.

When the massive ship rose out of the water and sailed above the waves, I threw aside my inhibitions and leaned across the railing to look down at the churning water.

"In a few minutes," Doc Treestone said, "the water will freeze, making it impossible for the ship to safely sail."

"I always wondered why the pirate ship would sail above the water," I said. "I guess I never put two and two together. Of course it couldn't sail in the icy water."

No sooner had I said the words than the temperature dropped a good fifteen degrees.

"Get on your coat and gloves," Sheriff Stiles said. "It's going to get even colder before we reach the island."

"That's my cue," Link said. "Can I burrow down in your pocket until we reach the island, Kara?"

I slipped on Bettina's coat and gloves. "You bet."

I unzipped the pocket and Link nestled down inside. It was strange going from a hot, eighty-degree summer day to freezing temperatures in a matter of fifteen minutes. I could see the island in the far distance and was about to yell out for Savage to look, when a huge tentacle reached out from the water and slapped down next to me on the railing.

"What the—"

Doc Treestone and Sheriff Stiles laughed.

"That's just Karl," Sheriff Stiles said.

I'd recently met Karl the Kraken during one of my evening swims in the ocean. A while back, Queen Atla had gifted me with the ability to remain underwater as a mermaid for an hour. So now I loved to go for swims whenever possible. Usually, I'm not fazed by what I see in the ocean, but the last swim had brought me face-to-face with Karl. And that had been intimidating.

"I know Karl," I said. "We've met before."

"Just saying hello, Valkyrie," Karl's deep, slow voice said inside my head.

The massive tentacle slowly uncurled itself from the railing and eased back down into the ocean. The fact we were a good six feet in the air left no doubt just how large Karl truly was.

"We should be at Winter Island shortly," Sheriff Stiles said.

"Is it a self-sustaining island?" I asked. "Or do most of the residents travel to Mystic Cove every day to work and shop?"

"It's relatively self-sustaining," Sheriff Stiles said. "Doc T would know more, of course. He grew up on Winter Island."

I glanced over at the polar bear shifter…and he waggled his bushy salt and pepper eyebrows at me.

"It's true," Doc Treestone said. "In fact, I still have family who live full time on Winter Island. I moved to Mystic Cove because it was just too much of a hassle to ferry back and forth all the time. Especially when I needed to get to the mainland fast. But Sheriff Stiles is correct. The island is self-sustaining. I'm not sure about the population. I'd say about a thousand or so supernaturals."

I nodded. Rota had said the same thing. "Are they all polar bear shifters or are there other types of supernaturals?"

"All sorts," Doc Treestone said. "There are polar bear, werewolf, and yeti shifters. Non-shifters include winter witches and winter fairies."

I frowned. "What exactly are winter witches and fairies?"

Doc Treestone smiled. "They can usually manipulate ice and snow."

"That's amazing," I said. "Hey, when does Barbie get back from her vacation?"

Barbie Warren was the forensic specialist for Mystic Cove. She was a six-foot-three descendant of the Amazon warrior tribe. When I wasn't sparring with Rota, I would practice fighting with Barbie.

"She should be back tomorrow night," Doc Treestone said. "I'll be happy when she returns. The lab has been extra quiet this week without her."

Barbie and two of her girlfriends had flown to Sailor's Bay, a paranormal island in the Caribbean, for a week-long vacation.

As we neared the island, the snow fell faster and harder. I flipped up the faux-fur hood on the down jacket Zahara had packed me and shoved my hands in the pockets.

"Och! Lass, I'm in here!" Link's voice called up to me.

"Oh! Sorry, Link," I said.

The boat descended, and I grabbed hold of the railing. But when we didn't hit the ice-packed water, I frowned in confusion.

"We won't touch the water," Doc Treestone said. "They'll stay back here so they can lower the ramp and it won't be a steep decline."

I reached down and scratched Savage under the chin. "C'mon, Savage. Hop down so I can get my bag."

Savage sighed, stood, and pushed his upper body out as far as it would go for a deep, long stretch. *"Give me a minute. I'm old. My body doesn't move that fast anymore."*

I snorted. "You're three. Not twenty-three."

Savage dropped to the floor of the ship and sashayed to the plank. Grabbing my carpetbag, I heaved it over my shoulder and followed him—Sheriff Stiles and Doc Treestone behind me.

At the bottom of the ramp, I took a right and headed down the dock, then carefully made my way up the slippery stairs… snow cascading down around me the entire time. When I finally reached the top of the stairs—my lungs burning from breathing in the frigid cold air—I stopped and got my first good look at the center of town.

Instead of a typical town with two-story buildings made of brick or old wood, this town had the look of a European winter village with wooden chalets as storefronts. The sloping roofs were covered with blankets of snow, and a few of the stores even had chimneys with curls of smoke floating into the air. I immediately wondered where all the holiday lights were…until I remembered it was technically still summer.

I strolled closer to the hustle and bustle of the town square and saw it was typical of other towns. There was an apothecary on the corner, a café and bakery across the street, a trendy boutique with winter clothes in another window storefront, a post office, and on down the road I could even see a sign pointing to a grocery store on the next street over. In the distance, snow-capped mountains flanked the town.

"What do you think, Kara?" Doc Treestone asked.

"It's beautiful," I said. "Looks like a postcard for Christmas. I keep forgetting it's actually summer and not winter."

A red and white snowmobile raced around the corner at the end of the street, narrowly missing the SUV pulling out from the curb. The two passengers waved and continued down the road.

"Will there be a way for me to get around on the island?" I asked. "Maybe a place I can rent a car?"

"Snowmobile," Sheriff Stiles and Doc Treestone both said simultaneously.

"Snowmobile," I said. "I can do that."

At least, I *hoped* I could do that. I'd never driven one before.

"I'm going to die on this island, aren't I?" Savage whined.

"I could get behind that," Link said jovially from my pocket.

"What's that?" Sheriff Stiles asked.

I shook my head. "Nothing. Link said something, but it wasn't important."

"It never is when he talks," Savage said.

Wanting to cut off the ensuing argument between Link and Savage before it could start, I turned to Doc Treestone. "How large is the island? Can I get around it in one day?"

Doc Treestone nodded and pointed to the right. "Down that street is a place to rent snowmobiles. It's fairly new in town from what my family has told me. And, yes. You can get from east to west side in about three hours, less time if you go north to south. Of course, that's assuming the snow isn't a hinderance."

"Do we know where the body is?" I asked.

"In the alley behind The Cozy Boutique," Sheriff Stiles said. "There's a volunteer law enforcement officer standing guard.

Retired. He should be back there making sure no one disturbs the scene."

Link popped out from inside my pocket and flittered around my head. "We'll need to notify next-of-kin when we get an ID."

"If it *is* Mya Harlan," Doc Treestone said, "then that will be Bonnie Harlan. Husband is deceased. Bonnie moved to a supernatural town somewhere in Florida, if I remember correctly. I knew Bonnie's parents. Went to school with her dad."

"I can do the notification to Mya's mom," Sheriff Stiles said.

"I'm sorry, Doc," I said. "I guess I should have known you'd probably know the family."

"I didn't know Mya," Doc Treestone said. "Truth be told, I hardly know any of the younger generation on the island anymore. Even if they are polar bear shifters."

We strolled past two more stores before turning down an alleyway, giving us a reprieve from the blowing snow. A big, burly man standing well over six feet ambled toward us, meeting us midway in the alley.

"Name's Rusty Tanner," he said, sticking out his hand for each of us, and then nodding to Link. "The woman who found Ms. Harlan's body is her roommate and the owner of The Cozy Boutique, Amber Slater."

"So we have a positive ID?" Sheriff Stiles mused.

Rusty nodded. "Yes. I mean, you can run her prints through your system, of course. But trust me when I say Mya Harlan was well known in these parts. Not always for good reasons."

"Meaning?" I asked.

Rusty frowned and rubbed his gloved hands over his head. "Well, let's just say Mya has had her fair share of trouble. Not so much the legal kind. More like the personal kind." Rusty looked down at my feet and blink. "You brought your cat with you?"

Savage looked up from grooming his paw. *"It's not exactly like I got a vote in the matter."*

"Long story," I said.

"Let's take a look at the body," Doc Treestone said.

Rusty whispered under his breath and conjured three sets of booties. As he did that, I set my bag down in the alley so I didn't disturb the crime scene. Rusty handed us the booties, and after donning them, we followed him toward the back alley.

"What did you mean when you said she'd had her fair share of personal trouble?" I asked as we neared the back alley.

"Oh, boyfriend troubles. Employment troubles. Didn't even have many girlfriends to hang out with from what I understand." We turned the corner to the back alley. "There she is."

I glanced over to where he gestured. Sure enough, a lone figure in a green parka and jeans lay face up on the snowy ground…an ice pick protruding from her neck.

3

"I'm no expert like the Doc here," Rusty said, "but I'm thinking maybe the ice pick through the neck is what killed her."

I bit back a smile. The sincere look on Rusty's face told me he wasn't being facetious or sarcastic. He was dead serious.

"Guess we won't need to find the murder weapon," Rusty continued. "Probably no fingerprints on it either, since you gotta wear gloves or risk frostbite." He held up his gloved hands. "But, again, I'm no doctor or forensics expert."

Doc Treestone nodded. "I'd have to say you're right about the murder weapon and the fingerprints."

Kudos to Doc T. He could have been snarky with his answer. But that didn't seem to be the nature of the kindly polar bear shifter.

"Well, isn't he a genius," Savage grumbled. *"Maybe you should see if you can't entice Rusty to join our crime-solving team."*

I couldn't say the same kind words for my sarcastic cat.

"Blood on her gloves," Sheriff Stiles said. "Looks like she tried to grab the pick out of her neck."

I squatted next to the body and examined it. Not only was there blood on her gloves, but also on her cheek and chin. She'd frantically tried to reach for the offensive weapon, but to no avail.

"I got another puncture wound," Doc said. "Looks like Mya was stabbed at least twice."

"What're you thinking?" Link asked, his wings buzzing in my ear.

"From the position of the ice pick," I said, "I'd say she saw her attacker. She staggers, trying to pull out the pick, maybe falls to her knees. You'd think she'd either pitch forward or to the side. But she's flat on her back."

"Someone moved the body?" Sheriff Stiles mused.

"Maybe." I glanced down at Mya's jacket. "I'll be interested to find out if Barbie discovers something on the jacket."

"Like a print?" Link asked.

I shrugged. "Or a substance. Maybe the killer kicked our victim backward with his or her foot. Could be something was transferred to the jacket from the sole of the shoe."

"Good thinking, Kara," Link said, his wings turning a vibrant purple.

"You say the roommate found her?" I asked.

"Yes, ma'am. Amber Slater. She's a winter fairy." He pointed to the building behind me. "That's her store there."

I stood and walked over to an overturned basket and customized coffee tumbler with Mya's name etched in pink and red. "With all this snow, I doubt we'll get shoe prints. Looks like our victim was delivering something."

"Yep," Rusty said. "Ms. Slater told me she was expecting Mya to deliver some lotions and stuff to her store."

"Let's start processing," I said. "I'd like to talk to Amber Slater as soon as possible."

Under Link's supervision, Rusty took photos while Doc Treestone examined the body and Sheriff Stiles and I processed the scene.

"I take it you are transporting the body back to Mystic Cove via the ship?" I asked.

"Yes," Doc Treestone said. "Sheriff Stiles can levitate her body for me, and then one of the fairies will meet me at the dock to transport Ms. Harlan to my lab." He stood and stepped back from the body. "I'm done here. Are you about finished, Kara?"

I nodded. "Just about. Sheriff, can you tape off the alley with crime scene tape for me real quick?"

"Of course."

"Thanks. I'm going to go inside and start my interviews." I nodded to Doc Treestone. "Thanks for your help. Keep me posted on the autopsy results."

"Will do," Doc T said. "And the minute Barbie gets back, I'll have her on the jacket, toiletries, coffee cup, and murder weapon. Don't forget to go around the corner and rent you a snowmobile. You'll need it to get around on the island."

"Will do. Thanks, Doc. Talk soon."

"If I can be of any more help to you," Rusty said, "you just let me know. I live above the bar over on Snowflake Lane. That's the street behind us where the snowmobile rental place is. I'm usually home most days."

"Thanks, Rusty," I said. "I'll take you up on that offer if I get stuck." I turned to Sheriff Stiles. "I'll keep you posted as well."

"Appreciate it," Sheriff Stiles said.

I motioned with my head for Link to follow me.

"Am I to assume I follow you?" Savage said dryly.

I rolled my eyes. "Yes, Savage. You can come along as well."

I heard Rusty ask Doc if I was talking to the cat, but I didn't wait around for Doc's reply. Bending down, I picked up my bag where I'd dropped it and headed for the front of the boutique.

I'd just stepped onto the sidewalk when I felt dozens of eyes on me. Looking around, I took in all the spectators. Some were watching from the windows of the other stores, other citizens were standing around outside, seemingly unaffected by the temperature and snow. It was like they were just waiting for a glimpse of something interesting. They didn't exactly look unfriendly, but they weren't smiling, either.

Doing my best to ignore the stares, I turned and strode the four steps to the front door of The Cozy Boutique. Pushing open the heavy wooden door, I winced at the garish chime that echoed in the silent store. When Link and Savage were inside, I let the door go and looked around.

"Hello. You must be the detective," the lady behind the counter said. "I'm Amber Slater, and this is my store."

4

Amber Slater looked to be in her mid-forties. With her wavy blonde hair, wide blue eyes, and delicate face, she all but screamed winter fairy.

"Let me just flip the sign to closed," Amber said as she hurried from behind the counter. "I didn't want you to think we were closed, so I left it open." She shook her head as she passed me. "It's been hard keeping everyone out. Trust me. This is the biggest thing to happen in…gosh, I don't know. Years, I'm sure." She flipped the sign over and pulled down the shade, leaning against the door. "I'm just a wreck. I can't believe this has happened."

"Here now, lass," Link said in his soothing Scottish brogue. "Dinna you worry none."

Amber gasped and pushed herself from the door. "Oh, a pixie. I'm sorry I didn't see you there. I'm just so nervous and upset." She curtsied. "How do you do?"

I couldn't tell if Amber Slater was for real…or if she was putting on a good show. Whatever it was, Link was eating it up.

"Now, now," Link said. "No need for formalities. I'm Link, and this is Detective Kara Hilder. And the mangy, four-legged beast is Savage."

Savage hissed and swiped his paw in the air, missing Link by a mile.

Amber giggled. "How delightful. Do you always have this many people helping you solve a crime, Detective Hilder?"

"Just my lucky day, is all," I said, setting my bag on the floor. "My usual partner, Zane, has been called away on another assignment. So Link will be helping me this time." I looked down at Savage. "And the three of us were in Mystic Cove visiting friends when I got the call about the bo—about Mya Harlan. So Savage had to come along."

"Well, I just love kitties, so he's welcome." She rushed past me again to retreat behind the counter. "I don't have a chair for you. I'm sorry."

"It's fine. May I call you Amber? Or do you prefer Ms. Slater?"

"Oh, call me Amber, please." She laughed and pressed her delicate hands to her chest. "Everyone does."

"Okay, Amber. I understand you know the deceased?"

Tears filled Amber's eyes. "I do. She rented a room from me. I own a house a couple streets over, and Mya has lived there for about five months now."

"Where did Mya live before that? Do you know?"

Amber cleared her throat and nodded. "Yes. She lived with her fiancé, but they broke up." She bit her lip and looked around the room. "Mya wasn't always the easiest person to get along with."

"What do you mean?" I asked.

Amber sighed. "Mya owed me like three months' back rent.

We weren't exactly friends." She plunked her head down onto the counter and groaned. "I know how that sounds."

"Rusty said you were expecting Mya," I said. "Can you tell me what that was about?"

Amber lifted her head. "Oh, yes. Since Mya owes me a lot of back rent, I told her she could sell her products here. You know, to recoup some of my losses? Anyway, she makes lotions and soaps and candles. Things of that nature. She was supposed to be here by noon, but when the noon hour passed and she didn't show, I just assumed she'd flaked on me. After finishing my lunch, I ran the trash outside to the back alley—I didn't want it to stink up my store—and as I was taking out the trash, that's when I saw her." Amber's chin trembled. "I was just so shocked. I ran over to her and was going to check to see if she was okay, but that's when I saw—" She broke off and swallowed hard. "That's when I saw the ice pick and the blood. And I knew."

"About what time was that, do you know?" I asked.

"I'd say maybe twelve-fifteen. I just had a tuna fish sandwich, so it wouldn't have taken more than fifteen minutes to eat."

"I can eat a can of tuna in less than two minutes," Savage said with a disdainful flick of his tail. *"She's obviously lying and hiding something."*

I barely refrained from rolling my eyes. "Can you tell me where Mya worked?"

"Well, she used to work at the apothecary in town, but she and Zelda had a major falling out about a month ago."

"What about?" Link asked as he landed on the counter.

Amber bit her lip. "Well, you'd have to ask Zelda, but from the rumors I heard, Mya tried to undercut Zelda. She started selling her own beauty products around town, and Zelda found out." She gave a small laugh. "Like how could Zelda not find out, right? It's not like Winter Island is a big place. Anyway,

Zelda found out Mya was selling her own line of products to people, and so she fired Mya. At that point, Mya already owed me like two months' rent, so I told her she could sell her stuff at my store. She still had yet to pay me, so I was going to tell her today when she dropped more product off that I was keeping a percentage of her earnings since she never offered to pay the back rent from what she earned."

"*I bet that made Amber here mad,*" Savage said. "*Mad enough to stab someone.*"

This time I didn't disagree with him. So far, Amber had admitted to Mya owing her back rent, and after giving Mya another helping hand, Mya *again* took advantage of Amber. I wasn't sure that was worth killing someone over, but it was a start.

"How much did she owe you?" Link asked.

"About twelve hundred dollars. So after Zelda fired Mya, she got a part-time job over at Snow Haven B&B working for Gwendolyn Morrowson." She leaned in close. "Which is how I know Mya at least had *some* income coming in. Between the products she sold here and her part-time job, she could at least offer to pay me something."

"Anyone else you can think of who might have it out for Mya?" I asked.

"I don't think so. But like I said, we weren't exactly friends. She was quite a bit younger than me, and she didn't confide in me about her life."

"I have to ask," I said. "Tell me where you were today from eleven-thirty until you discovered the body around twelve-fifteen?"

Amber's eyes went wide. "Am I a suspect? But I'm the one who discovered the body. Why would I call it in if I killed her?"

"Just a routine question," Link assured her.

"Lie," Savage hissed. *"Even I know she's a suspect, and I didn't go to some fancy school for detective training."*

"I was here, at my store," Amber said. "I opened at ten this morning, and then I just waited until noon for Mya to stop by. I had like two or three customers today." She threw up her hands. "I didn't go anywhere. I just stayed here in my store."

"Thank you, Amber," I said. "I think that's all the questions we have right now. Can you give me your address and phone number? I'd like to stop by at some point and look around Mya's bedroom."

"Of course." Amber picked up a pen and scribbled her name, address, and phone number on a piece of paper before handing it to me. "Here you go. What about…" She gestured toward the back door that led to the alleyway. "Should I just lock the back door and not go out there?"

I nodded and slipped her info into my jeans pocket. "Yes. Back alley is off limits until I release it."

"Okay. I walk to work most days anyway, so that's not a problem. Throwing out the trash is the only reason I go back there. Um…I guess you'll keep me posted?"

"I'm sure we'll be in touch again," I said vaguely as I bent to pick up my carpetbag. "Right now, I need to go pick up my snowmobile and then head over to Snow Haven to check in."

Amber blinked in surprise. "Oh, you're staying at the place Mya worked?"

"Small world," I said. "Why don't you close up shop and go home? You've had a hard day."

Amber nodded and sighed. "I probably will. Only people who'll come in will be gossipers wanting to know what you asked and what all I know. Which isn't much. No one's gonna really want to buy anything today."

I said goodbye, then quietly shut the front door behind me when Link and Savage exited as well.

"They say the person who finds the body is often the killer," Link said. "Which is a shame because I liked the girl."

I laughed and strode down the snowy sidewalk, careful not to make eye contact with anyone. "Don't accuse her just yet. Seems we have some other good leads to check out."

"I need a cat nap and some food soon," Savage grumbled as he sashayed down the sidewalk in front of me.

"Soon," I said. "But before we talk to Zelda at the apothecary, let's go get a snowmobile and check in at the B&B."

5

Snowmobile & Gear was just one street over. Before reaching for the front door, I peeked inside the window and saw two men in a heated exchange. One was dressed casually in colorful winter gear, while the other was more polished in tailored pants and designer coat.

I pushed the door open and was surprised when no bell alerted my presence.

"I'm doing the best I can," the casually dressed man said. "You can't get blood from a turnip."

"Sounds like trouble," Link whispered.

"I want my money, Brody," the well-dressed man said. "Don't make me take the next step. You won't like it."

"Are you threatening me? Because if you are, I'd tell you to go lean on my partner, but we both know that's not going to do you any good." The casually dressed man turned and caught sight of Link, Savage, and me standing near the front door. He put on a huge, fake smile and stepped away from the other man.

"Welcome to Snowmobile & Gear. I'm Brody Billings, the owner. What can I get for you today?"

"We'll finish this another time," the other man said, turning his ice-blue eyes on me. "Good afternoon."

"Good afternoon," I said. "I hope I'm not interrupting anything."

"Nothing that can't wait," the well-dressed Yeti shifter said before turning back to Brody. "I'll see you tomorrow."

I stepped aside and let the man pass before turning to Brody. "I need to rent a snowmobile."

"You've come to the right place." He glanced at Link and then Savage. "I don't have helmets small enough to fit your pets."

Link's wings turned black as he whipped out his tiny-but-sharp sword from his side. "I'm no one's pet, lad. Best ye remember that."

Brody held up his hands. "Sorry, dude."

"If I wasn't so puny from hunger, I'd scratch out his eyes."

"Link is my partner," I said. "And Savage is…well, he's his own animal. And they both already have helmets."

"Seriously?" Brody said. "I didn't know they made helmets that small. That's cool, man. You ride?"

"I ride a Ducati."

Brody's eyes widened. "Sweet. I've always wanted to ride one. I hear they're fast."

"I love mine. But it's back in Mystic Cove, which is why I need a snowmobile."

Brody nodded. "Right. You must be here because of what happened over on Main Street. Word travels fast around these parts." He shoved his hands in his pockets as he strolled behind the counter. "Do you know anything yet? Like how she died? Or maybe who killed her?"

"Did you know the deceased?" I asked.

"I did." Brody slid a form across the counter to me. "I need you to fill out and sign the paperwork."

It took just a few minutes to complete the paperwork, and once that was done, he handed me a set of keys.

"Have you ever driven a snowmobile before?"

"I haven't," I said.

"Come out back and let me give you a lesson real quick."

I hitched my carpetbag higher on my shoulder as Link, Savage, and I followed Brody to the back of the store and out the door into an alleyway just like the one Mya had been murdered in. Unlike the previous alleyway, this one didn't have a dead body…only about eight snowmobiles lined up in a row.

"You definitely have enough to choose from," I said. "I was worried you might be sold out."

Brody snorted. "Not hardly. I get the occasional tourist in here wanting to rent, but I didn't think out my business plan a whole lot before I opened the place." He gave me a sheepish look. "Most citizens already own their own snowmobiles."

I nodded. "I can see how that might be a problem. So, what do I need to know?"

Brody spent the next few minutes showing me how to start, stop, and steer. When he finished, I unzipped my bag and took out Link's helmet and tossed it to him while I strapped on Savage's.

"This is so humiliating," Savage said.

"It may just save your life," I said.

When I finished, I turned back to Brody.

"I put down I'd need the vehicle at least two days."

He waved his hand in the air dismissively. "If you need it longer, it's no problem." He gestured to the row of snowmobiles beside us. "There's plenty for others to rent."

"I'll be staying at Snow Haven B&B," I said. "Can you give me directions?"

"Of course." Brody laid out the quickest way for me to get to the house. "It's a five-minute walk from here, so it'll take you no time to get there on the snowmobile. It's a nice place to stay, from what I hear." He cleared his throat. "Listen, you wanna go get a drink or something later? I can show you where most citizens hang out at night and drink."

I snorted. "Is drinking what people do here at night?"

He shrugged. "Not much else to do. Whaddya say? Want to meet me at the local watering hole later?"

"Let's go, Kara," Link said. "We don't have time for this."

I smiled at Brody. "Sorry. It was nice of you to ask, but I'm not here to socialize. I'm here to solve a murder. Plus, I have a boyfriend, and trust me, the fallen angel isn't anyone you'd want to tangle with."

Brody's eyes went wide. "You're dating Zane?"

"You know him?" I asked.

"Uh, no. I've never met him, but he's legendary around here. Even on Winter Island. Not many fallen angels live around here."

"I see. Well, now you understand why I'll have to say no. I'm here to do a job."

Brody nodded. "Yeah, I get it. I figured you'd be seeing someone, anyway." He shrugged and grinned. "But I had to ask."

I thanked him and patted my pocket for Link. Saluting me, Link slipped down inside my coat pocket as I settled down onto the padded seat, shifting my bag higher up my back. Once I was on, Savage jumped on behind me and settled down as well.

"Hold on tight," I yelled to Savage.

With a final wave to Brody, I slowly started down the back alley. When we reached the end of the street, I made a right and drove toward Snow Haven B&B.

The town was laid out in typical fashion, with storefronts along the main streets, and the houses branching off from there. Most of the houses were Tudor and Chateau homes, just scaled way down. Cottages were sprinkled here and there, but mostly, it was like driving through a town in the Swiss Alps. I took another right on Winter Drive and headed for the large Tudor at the end of the lane.

I parked next to another snowmobile and shut off the engine. Link popped out of my pocket and looked around—purple pixie dust leaking from a wing.

"Peaceful," he murmured.

The two-story Tudor was comprised of half-timbered wooden beams set against white stucco, with herringbone brickwork near the top. The roof was steeply pitched and covered in slate tiles encasing two chimneys. My favorite part of the house, though, were the windows. The façade and the side of the house I could see had two bay windows, four narrow windows with diamond-shaped panes, and even a couple dormer windows near the roof.

"It definitely has that elegant old-world charm," I said.

"It'll do," Savage said as he jumped off the snowmobile.

I rolled my eyes and headed for the ornate wooden front door. Before I could ring the bell, a tall woman with flaming red hair opened the door and smiled at us.

"Hello," she said, gesturing me inside. "My name is Gwendolyn Morrowson, and this is my home. You must be the detective staying here?"

I nodded and gestured to Link. "I am, and this is my partner for the investigation, Link."

Link dipped his wings. "Nice to meet you, lass."

The pretty witch smiled. "Lovely to meet you as well, Mr. Link." She looked down at Savage. "And who is this lovely cat?"

Ignoring Link's snort and Savage's hiss, I glared down at the feline. "This is Savage. I hope it's okay he stays? I was in town when I got the call and didn't have time to go back to my cottage to drop him off."

"Of course," Gwendolyn said. "All animals are welcome." She chuckled. "Both the Supernatural kind and the non-supernatural kind. Come, let me give you a quick tour and then show you to your room. I'm sure you have lots to do." She sighed. "Such a shame about Mya."

"I'll want to interview you once I settle in," I said.

"Of course." She motioned around her. "This is the foyer, and as you can see, the stairs are directly behind me, and to my right is the living room."

The foyer was a mix of rustic elegance. The polished wooden floor gleamed from both the overhead chandelier lighting and the light reflecting from the leaded windows. On the antique oak table pushed against the wall was a guest registry book, a bowl of mints, and fresh flowers.

We bypassed the curved staircase and entered the living room. My eye was immediately drawn to the massive stone fireplace taking up one wall. A roaring fire was burning inside. Two plush couches in sage green, three brown armchairs, and dozens of crocheted blankets gave the room a cozy feel. Glancing out the bay window, I could see the backdrop of the snow-covered mountains.

I strolled over to the cuckoo clock on the wall. "Does it work?"

"It does," Gwendolyn said. "It belonged to my great-great-grandfather."

I turned back to face her. "I can't wait to hear and see it in action."

"Unless I can eat the bird that pops out, I'll pass on the display."

I surreptitiously glanced at Gwendolyn, making sure she wasn't a witch who could communicate with animals. I didn't think she'd find Savage as amusing as he found himself. When she didn't react, I shifted the bag on my shoulder and stepped away from the clock.

"Through here is the library," she said, passing under another archway. "You are welcome to grab a book and read, of course. But I doubt you'll have much time. There's also a place to play chess or checkers."

Three dark walnut bookshelves lined the room, each filled with myriad books, a couple family photos, and small knick-knacks. A roll-top desk was against one wall overlooking the side yard. In the center of the room, facing another smaller fireplace, were four leather armchairs and two floor lamps.

"This room is inviting," I said. "I just want to stay here, curl up by the fire, and read all day."

Gwendolyn smiled. "Good. That's what it's supposed to make you want to do." We stepped out into a hallway. "Through that archway is the formal dining room and kitchen. I offer a buffet-style breakfast in the mornings, but lunches and dinners are on your own. If you need hot tea or coffee throughout the day, just ring, and I will bring it up for you." She gestured for me to head toward the steps. "Let's get you settled into your own room so you can get started."

At the bottom of the stairs, I stepped back so she could lead the way. When we got partway up the stairs, another couple descended from the second floor. Luckily, the staircase was wide enough to handle us all.

"My wife and I are heading into town to do some shopping," the dark-haired werewolf said. "Can you suggest a place for afternoon tea?"

"Tabitha's Tea Shoppe," Gwendolyn said. "She's a talented kitchen witch who makes her own blends and pastries."

"Excellent," the werewolf said. "Doesn't that sound wonderful, darling?"

The woman nodded. "Sounds superb."

"Are you staying here as well?" the man asked me.

I nodded. "Yes. A couple days, at least."

"Well," he said, "you'll enjoy it here."

They continued down the stairs, and I followed Gwendolyn up to the second floor.

"I have four bedrooms upstairs," Gwendolyn said, "but only two are rented this week, including you. So you should have adequate privacy, and you are free to come and go as you please." She stopped at a door in the hallway. "This is your bedroom. Go ahead and settle in, and then come downstairs when you'd like to talk." She pushed open the door and smiled. "Let me know if you need anything else when you come downstairs."

I watched her walk away, then turned to enter my room.

"I'm keen on the décor," Link said. "I like a touch of the outdoors brought in, and she's done it with this home."

I smiled. "Of course you would. You live in a tree stump."

Link grinned. "Don't knock it until you've tried it."

"Pass," Savage said. *"But I will take a nap if that won't put anyone out too much."*

I snorted. "Yes. You stay here and nap. Link and I will conduct interviews."

I dropped my bag onto the queen-sized bed and looked around. An antique armoire was pushed against the wall directly opposite the bed. I strolled over to the French doors and looked out. My breathtaking view was of the snow-capped mountains in the distance.

"This view is amazing," I said.

"You think that's amazing?" Link mused. "Come look at this bathroom."

I turned from the doors and smiled. "That good, huh?"

"There's a clawfoot tub in here," Link said. "I may never want to leave."

"Don't tease me like that," Savage said as he leaped up onto the bed.

I laughed. "Knock it off, Savage. Take your nap."

"Could you at least leave me a crumb of food before you go? I prefer not to starve to death."

Link snorted as he flew over and landed on a down pillow. "You're looking pretty plump these days. I doubt you'd starve."

I bit back a grin. "I'll go see what our hostess can spare."

Savage closed his eyes. *"That would be acceptable."*

6

"Thank you, Gwendolyn." I took the tin of gourmet cat food she offered. "I'm sure Savage will love this."

"It's no problem at all," she said. "I always keep pet food around. Now, sit down and let's talk."

I pulled out a chair from the kitchen table and waited to speak until she'd poured the tea she'd been brewing into two cups. Link was perched on the counter eating a peanut butter cookie that had been cut in half.

Stirring in a spoonful of honey, I picked up the cup and blew across the top. "How many employees do you have outside of Mya Harlan?"

"Just two." Gwendolyn shook her head. "I mean one. There's me, Abby Sellars, and Mya. Abby and Mya took turns cleaning. Today was Mya's day to work. I do all the cooking." She smiled. "Kitchen witch. It comes naturally."

"I've been getting better at picking up on what kind of supernatural people are," I said. "I didn't *think* you were a winter witch, but I wasn't sure."

She took a sip of her tea. "No. I'm actually a transplant from Mystic Cove. I moved to Winter Island and opened this B&B about eight years ago."

"How long had Mya worked for you?" I asked.

"Not long. Maybe a month. I was actually friends with Mya's mother before she moved away a few years back. So when Mya came to me about four weeks ago asking for employment, I couldn't say no." She sighed and picked up a peanut butter cookie from the plate. "Mya had a hard time keeping a job." She snorted. "And friends." She shook her head and bit into the cookie. "I don't know why that was. She was just argumentative and…impulsive? Flighty? Selfish? Take your pick."

I grabbed a cookie from the tray. "So not well liked?"

Gwendolyn shook her head. "Exactly. The reason why she needed a job was because her employer, Zelda Yarnell, had fired her. Zelda owns the apothecary in town. She found out Mya was making her own products and selling them at a lower price to other store owners in town."

I frowned. "Didn't Mya realize Zelda would find out?"

Gwendolyn shrugged. "I'm not sure Mya cared. So anyway, I hired Mya, *and* I started buying my toiletries for the rooms from her." She sighed. "Which did not make Zelda happy, but what could I do?" She shoved the last of the cookie in her mouth, chewed, then swallowed. "The truth is, Detective, I didn't know Mya that well. I just couldn't warm to her. She was *nothing* like her mother. Her mom is kind, sweet, warm, caring." She shrugged and took a sip of her hot tea. "I don't know where Mya got her disposition. I guess from her father." She smiled. "I didn't know him at all. He died before I moved to Winter Island." The smile left her face. "This will devastate Mya's mom." She bit her lip. "Has she been told?"

I nodded. "The sheriff is taking care of that. Tell me what happened today. Mya was working here?"

"Yes. She'd asked to take a basket of soaps and lotions to Amber Slater over at The Cozy Boutique. She left around eleven-thirty and said she'd be back by noon or a little after. I told her that was fine. She only had the one bedroom and bathroom to clean, so most of her morning was spent tidying up in the living room and library." She shrugged. "That's it. She left, and when the twelve o'clock hour passed, I didn't really think anything about it. But when fifteen more minutes passed, and Mya still wasn't back, I started to wonder what happened. I wasn't exactly worried, of course. Just more put out." She winced. "I know that sounds bad. But it doesn't take more than ten minutes to walk to the boutique."

"I understand. You say you were here the entire time?"

"Oh, yes."

"Did you talk to anyone?" I asked.

"Not really. The couple you met on the stairs earlier was still in the house. I could hear them walking around upstairs. But that's about it."

I nodded. "I take it Zelda Yarnell knew about Mya selling to Amber Slater over at The Cozy Boutique?"

I already knew the answer, but I was curious to see what Gwendolyn knew.

"Oh, yes. Zelda isn't happy with me or Amber. Or really anyone who has been buying from Mya." She took another drink of her tea and sighed. "Zelda has made her displeasure known."

"So I'll obviously need to talk to Zelda Yarnell," I said. "Anyone else?"

"Mya's ex-fiancé. They've had quite the row the last few months."

"Tell me about that."

Link flew over to the table and picked up the other half of his cookie. "These are delicious."

"Thank you," Gwendolyn said. "My mother's recipe."

I ate the last of my cookie. "Mya's ex?"

"Oh, right. Now, I don't know the entire story because Mya never volunteered, so all I got was gossip. But I guess Mya and her ex took out a huge loan and Mya just up and bailed on it and him."

"How large of a loan are we talking?" I mused.

"About thirty thousand if the rumors are true."

Link whistled. "That's a pretty good motive."

"I can't see Brody killing Mya," Gwendolyn said. "He honestly seemed to care about her. They were engaged. Well, that is until Mya left him and the business."

I held up my hand. "Wait. Are you telling me Mya was engaged to Brody Billings? The guy who runs the snowmobile place?"

"You know him?" Gwendolyn asked.

I snorted. "Yeah. And he said he knew Mya, but he didn't act like he *knew* Mya." I pushed back from the table. "Thank you for talking with me. I'm going to head out and do some investigating."

She slid a keyring across the table with two keys attached. "One unlocks your room, the other unlocks the front door. A word of caution, though. Winter Island is a magical island. It snows constantly, but it doesn't really stick. But by seven o'clock every night, the snow changes, and we get blizzard-like accumulation. It snows anywhere from six inches to a foot each night. If you aren't used to that kind of weather, it would be best if you completed your work by seven and stayed in the rest of the evening. "

"That's a lot of snow," I said. "How do you do it day in and day out?"

Gwendolyn smiled. "You get used to it after a while. Oh, and if you have a reason to go near the mountain, please be careful. There are reports of small avalanches at least every other day. Nothing catastrophic, but you could get trapped or lost easily enough."

"Thank you for the warnings," I said. "C'mon Link. I'll feed Savage real quick, and then we'll get to work."

7

"Since the apothecary is first on the street, let's stop here," I said, taking off my helmet. "Interview Zelda Yarnell."

"I'm still mighty suspicious of that Brody Billings fella," Link said as he dropped his hollowed-out walnut shell helmet onto the seat of the snowmobile. "He knew all along who Mya was, and then he had the nerve to ask you out!"

"Plus, I doubt it was the first time the blue-eyed man in the store told Brody he better pay up or else. It could be when Brody realized he couldn't pay back the loan he and Mya had taken out, he took his anger out on Mya."

I stepped up onto the sidewalk and headed for the apothecary, Winter's Blend. Pushing open the front door, overhead bells jangled as I stepped inside. There were two customers milling around the back of the store.

"One moment," a female voice called out. "I'll be right there."

Link flew over to one of the shelves and scanned the products. "Think I should buy Lily one of these? Would she like it?"

I smiled. "I think that's a lovely idea. It's getting pretty serious between you two."

Link flushed, and he turned to read the labels on the front of the bottles. "Aye, it's a wee bit serious, lass."

"I bet your sister loves that," I joked. "Her best friend and her brother."

"She's beside herself with glee. And she's not the only one puttin' pressure on me. Me own Mam is houndin' me somethin' fierce."

I laughed. "I think Lily is perfect. She's gentle and sweet, and she puts up with you."

Link smiled and ducked his head. "Aye. A pixie could do worse, that's true."

I wandered over to the window and read the purple flyer. The Monthly Winter Run was the first Saturday of the month. That was just two days by my calculation. All supernatural shifters were welcome to run. There was also a reminder that stores would be open later than usual, and witches and fairies would sell homemade goods in the park on the square.

"Sorry to keep you waiting," a woman said as she hurried from out of the back room. "How can I…" She trailed off when she caught sight of us. "You must be the detectives."

"How did you know?" I asked.

She glanced back at the two browsing customers before leaning forward. "Word travels fast in these parts. I heard a female and her pixie were here to find out what happened to Mya." She frowned. "Someone got it wrong, though. They said a cat was helping you as well."

I bit back a grin. Savage would blow a gasket if he was expected to help investigate the case. "I came with a cat, but he's not here right now."

"I know why you're here," Zelda said, motioning us over to

the register. "You want to talk about Mya's murder. I'm sure you've already heard I fired her about a month ago."

"We heard that, yes," I said.

Zelda crossed her arms over her chest and scowled. "I had no choice." She raised one hand in the air. "She left me no choice!"

She must have recognized how loud she'd gotten because Zelda shot another glance back at the customers.

"Why don't you tell me what happened?" I said in my most soothing tone.

Zelda sighed and dropped her arms. "Fine. As you've already learned, you can't do anything in this town without someone immediately knowing. The morning I fired Mya, I'd already had a store owner call me and say Mya had been in trying to push her own beauty and healthcare products. And did I know about it? Of course I didn't! So when Mya walked in, I was already fired up. I was about to jump her when the front door opened and in walked Lila Vaughn."

"And who is Lila Vaughn?" I asked.

"Well, she used to be Lila Thornton, but she got married a few months ago. Anyway, that's what the fight was about. I guess Mya had promised Lila a ton of beauty products for her bridesmaids, and Lila had even paid Mya a huge down payment, but Mya never delivered on the goods. Lila wanted her money back."

"What ended up happening?" I mused.

"I asked Lila to leave and settle the matter elsewhere. I didn't want arguing in my store. I then turned to Mya and promptly fired her." She smiled. "Which made Lila happy. But I don't know what happened after they both left."

"And this was about a month ago, you say?" I asked.

"Yes."

I nodded. "Okay. And how long had Mya worked here before you fired her?"

"A little over a year. But Lila wasn't the only one who hated Mya."

"Who else should we talk to?" Link asked.

The two ladies who'd been shopping chose that moment to head to the register. They slowed as they neared us, so I smiled and turned to study a mountain of soaps to my right, giving them some privacy. Once the transaction was completed, and the two ladies hurried out the door, I turned back to Zelda.

"I can think of two other people," Zelda said as though we'd never been interrupted. "One is her ex-fiancé, Brody Billings. The other is this girl named Jessica Weston."

"We know about Brody Billings," I said. "Why Jessica Weston?"

Zelda snorted. "Where to start? Mya and Jessica went to school here on the island. As I'm sure you can imagine having seen most of the town, there aren't a lot of students in a class. I attended school here and my graduating class had five."

"Wow," I said. "That does seem small."

I'd been homeschooled, so I never attended public school. Mystic Cove had a paranormal school, which I knew differed from public schools in the human world. Or, at least, the curriculum was different.

Zelda let out a small bark of laughter. "Yeah, that's small. Our class reunions are held across the street at the café. Anyway, Mya was—I don't know. She wasn't exactly a bully, but she could be mean and self-centered. She always assumed others were here to see to her whims. Does that make sense?"

I nodded. "It does."

"Okay, so I don't know what all went on between Mya and Jessica, but it was well known throughout town those two didn't care for each other. And the thing is, I've spoken to Jessica a ton of times, and she's just the sweetest girl." Zelda shrugged. "And maybe that's part of it. Maybe Mya sensed that shyness from Jessica and exploited it."

"Then Mya was a bully," Link said.

"I guess you're right," Zelda said. "Mya was just careful about it."

"Do you know where Lila Vaughn and Jessica Weston live?" I asked.

"Sure. Lila lives on the other side of the mountain. Like *way* out. It'll probably take you a good hour in this weather to get there. She and her husband, Bruno, got married four months ago on Valentine's Day. His family owns the ski resort outside of town. I know Bruno runs the facility, and I think Lila still works from home. I don't totally understand what she does, but it's some kind of marketing. I know that."

"And Jessica?" I mused.

"Oh, she's right here in town. Over off Snowcap Drive. Shouldn't take you but five minutes to get there from here."

"Great. I'll pull up their addresses when I get back to the B&B."

Zelda rolled her eyes. "The B&B. That's another account I lost thanks to Mya. Although, now that she's dead, I suppose I could get Gwendolyn back as a client."

"I suspect you could," Link said.

I bit back a smile. "I need to know where you were today from eleven-thirty to twelve-thirty."

"Right here." She motioned around her store. "I usually close for half an hour to eat my lunch—a lot of stores in town do that—so from twelve to twelve-thirty, I was inside my store eating lunch. I never left."

"Did you have any customers from eleven-thirty to noon?" I asked.

Zelda narrowed her eyes. "I'm not sure."

"Maybe you can check your receipts?" Link suggested. "That might jog your memory."

I tried not to smile at the helpful suggestion that wasn't exactly phrased as a suggestion. "Yes, that might help."

"I don't have to look," Zelda said. "It was a slow morning. My last customer was around eleven today. She bought three bars of soap and some lotion."

"So you were alone from eleven until twelve-thirty?" I asked.

"Yes," Zelda said between clenched teeth. "But I didn't kill Mya. In fact, I've given you three different suspects."

"Yes," Link said. "You've certainly given us plenty of others to look at for the murder."

"One last question," I said. "When was the last time you spoke to Mya?"

"When I fired her a month ago," Zelda said.

8

"You nearly made me laugh out loud with your 'other suspects' comment," I said to Link as we headed for Brody Billings' snowmobile rental store on the next street over. "I mean, it was obvious what she was doing, but the fact you pointed it out was fierce."

Link grinned at me, his wings glowing bright green. "Thank ye, lass. I have me moments."

Chuckling, I sidestepped an enormous pile of snow near the curb and nodded hello to a passerby. She didn't return my greeting. Not that I expected her to. Most small towns weren't unfriendly. They were just…guarded. It was scary to think something horrible could happen to someone they knew who lived in their general vicinity.

"I could use a jolt of caffeine," I said. "Maybe after we talk to Brody, we should stop by the café to warm up and get some coffee and a snack?"

"Sounds good. I could use some hot milk and honey."

When we reached Brody's business, I pushed open the front

door and stepped inside the empty store. Brody looked up from behind the counter and grimaced.

"I wasn't hiding anything," he said. "I just didn't think I should volunteer anything."

I narrowed my gaze. "Well, that just makes me think you have something to hide."

Link zipped over to the counter and crossed his arms over his puffy pink and yellow coat. "Yeah, that makes us think you have something to hide."

Brody threw up his hands. "What did you want me to say? 'Yeah, the dead body in the alleyway is my ex-girlfriend.'"

"Let's start there," I said, glancing around the store. "I'd ask if you want to take this somewhere more private, but customers aren't exactly beating down your door."

Brodie's nostrils flared. "I told you, I didn't exactly think this business endeavor through."

"You dated the deceased, Mya Harlan?" I asked.

He nodded. "Yes. For almost a year. In fact, we were engaged."

"What happened?"

He made a sound of disgust. "What happened is we went into business together, and she flaked."

"This business?" I asked, waving a hand in the air.

"Yes. About eight months ago, we agreed we would go in half for the loan. We took out a thirty-thousand dollar loan, but I would be responsible for fifteen thousand, and she would be responsible for fifteen thousand. That's what we agreed on. What I didn't know was that at the first sign of hardship, she would bail, leaving me to repay the full thirty-thousand dollars. She left me here high and dry and moved out of our apartment."

"Which bank do you have your loan through?" I asked.

Brody's lips went flat, and he looked away. "I didn't go

through a bank. I asked my cousin for a loan, and he gave it to me."

"Was he the gentleman who was in here earlier?" I asked.

A muscle jumped in Brody's cheek. "That was him. He's demanding a payment, and I'm having a hard time coming up with it. No big deal."

Link shook his head and landed on the counter. "Boy, don't you know you never go into business with family?"

"I do now."

"Does your cousin live in town?" I asked.

Brody shook his head. "No. And it's not like he couldn't afford it. His parents own the ski resort outside of town here. I also work there part-time as a ski instructor. Trust me, he had the money to loan me. And he'd never have gone off on me had Mya not screwed his wife over."

"How did she do that?" I asked.

Brody snorted. "She didn't deliver on a promise. Which was sort of Mya's modus operandi. And so that meant the new wife put the screws to Bruno, and he applied pressure to me."

It suddenly all made sense. "Is his wife's name Lila?"

Brody's eyes went wide. "Yeah. How did you know?"

"She's smart like that," Link said, pink pixie dust leaking from one wing. "I taught her everything she knows."

I couldn't help but grin. "Let's talk about Mya, and the last time you saw or spoke to her."

"It's been a couple of days."

"Okay, let's talk specifically about today," I said. "Where were you from eleven-thirty until twelve-thirty?"

Brody crossed his arms over his chest. "I worked this morning up at the resort. I gave a ski lesson until eleven. I'm not the least bit ashamed to say I ducked out as soon as I could so I didn't have to talk to Bruno. Takes about thirty minutes to get into town from the resort, so I probably got back to town around eleven-thirty or eleven-forty. I came to the store and placed a takeout order at the café. They said it would be ready around twelve-fifteen."

"What did you do for those thirty minutes?" I asked.

"Well, I mean, I just hung out. I don't open the shop until twelve-thirty because most shopkeepers close from twelve to twelve-thirty. So I called in my order, and then took a walk to blow off steam because I was worked up over having to ditch Bruno. So I probably walked around town for twenty minutes. I then stopped by the café, picked up my meal, then came straight back here."

I narrowed my eyes. "And did you see Mya during this winter walkabout?"

Link chuckled. "Winter walkabout."

Brody scowled. "No. I never saw her."

"Do you know of anybody else who might have wanted to hurt Mya?"

"Besides me, you mean?"

"You said it," Link said.

Brody looked at the wall behind my shoulder and shrugged. "Plenty. Mya knew this girl—I think she's real nice, just introverted—but Mya had it out for her for some reason. Her name is Jessica Weston. She lives on the outskirts of town off Snowcap Drive." He threw up one hand. "And I already told you about my cousin's wife being pissed at her. Mya was supposed to make this big elaborate gift for each of her bridesmaids, took Lila's money, and then never delivered the products." He thumped his chest with his fist. "And, somehow, that is also my fault."

"Anyone else?" I asked.

"I assume. You've spoken to Zelda Yarnell?" he mused.

I nodded. "Yes."

Brody shrugged. "Then I guess that's everyone."

"Thank you for your time," I said. "If we have further questions, we know where you work."

"How's that snowmobile working out for you?" he asked tersely.

"Working just fine," I said.

Link and I didn't say anything else until we exited the store.

"You're telling me in a town this small," Link said as he hovered near my shoulder, "that Brody never once saw Mya during his thirty-minute walk. Do you believe that?"

I shook my head. "I really don't."

"Me neither. Brody seems to be good at hiding things and lying. He's even doing it with his cousin. Makes me wonder if anything he told us was the truth."

"Let's hit the bakery instead of the café and get something hot to drink. Should be quicker that way, and then we can go talk to Jessica Weston."

9

After grabbing a double mocha, a hot milk and honey, and two scones from the bakery, I asked a couple different locals where Snowcap Drive was located. I figured even if I got two or three different versions of how to get there, I'd still know where I was going.

Turned out, there was only one way to get there.

As the snowmobile bumped along the narrow lane on the outskirts of town, I glanced at my watch. It was almost five o'clock. My plan was to question Jessica, grab something more substantial than a scone at the café, and then get back to the B&B before the seven o'clock blizzard started.

I slowed down when I came to a driveway with a mailbox that read 'Weston' on the side. A small sign next to the mailbox read 'Weston Mushroom Farm.' Figuring this to be the place, I turned into the driveway and drove the thirty yards to the house.

Or should I say the tiny hut?

The round home was no more than four hundred square feet. It almost looked like a hobbit home—complete with the round windows and round door. The roof was covered in what I assumed was some kind of moss, and creeping vines snaked their way around the hut.

"Reminds me of me own childhood stump when I was a lad," Link said as he popped out of my winter coat and unhooked his walnut-shell helmet. "Now I'm a wee bit homesick."

I smiled and set my helmet on the seat next to his. "Perfectly understandable."

Before I could reach the round door and knock, it was opened by a curly-haired girl with a long face and round glasses. Her shoulder-length brown hair looked like it hadn't been brushed in days.

"Yes?" she said. "Are you here for mushrooms?"

"No. My name is Detective Hilder, and this is my partner, Link. We need to speak to you about Mya Harlan."

"Mya? Did she accuse me of something? Because let me tell you, it's the other way around. That woman has done nothing but torment me for years."

I held up my hand. "Could we come in? It's rather cold out here, and I'm not used to the weather."

"Oh, of course." She pushed her glasses up her nose. "I'm sorry. How rude of me." She stepped back and motioned us inside. "It's cramped, but it works for me."

I crossed the threshold and was immediately bombarded with the scent of damp wood and the earthy aroma of mushrooms. All around the hut, makeshift crates were stacked at least three feet high. In between the slats, I could make out the mushrooms nestled inside.

"It's quaint," I said.

"Thank you. I grew up in this house. When my parents moved off the island, they gave it to me. Why don't we go to the kitchen and have some coffee? It's my own special blend."

It was on the tip of my tongue to tell her no, that I'd just had a mocha...but I'd found in my years of investigating that people often let things slip over a cup of joe.

"I'd love a cup of coffee," I lied.

I followed her to the back of the hut. A mini-fridge, sink, two-burner stove, wooden slats for shelves, and a large wooden table made up the kitchen. Pulling out a rickety chair, I gingerly sat down. Link perched on the back of the chair next to me.

"This is my best seller," Jessica said. "It has shiitake, oyster, turkey tail, lion's main, reishi, and a couple other magical mushroom ingredients."

I blinked in surprise. "Is this a mushroom drink? I thought you said it was coffee?"

Jessica laughed. "Trust me. You'll like this more than you like coffee."

I wasn't as confident as Jessica, but I didn't want to be rude.

"If those crates are in your way, just move them to the floor," Jessica said as she added a brown powder to two mugs. "I'll deliver those tomorrow to residence on the island."

"You're a mushroom farmer?" I asked.

"Sure am. I also make products from them. I make this coffee. I also make a mushroom tea blend, a powdered mushroom soup mix, and a couple other mushroom products."

Jessica carried the two mugs back to the table, setting one down in front of me and the other directly across from me. "Did you want a small glass, Link?"

Link nodded. "I might try a small thimble, yes."

"I've never prepared a glass that small," Jessica admitted, "but I'm sure I could get the proportions right."

"Here." I pushed my cup away from me. "Don't go to all that trouble. Just spoon out some of mine. I just had a large coffee from the bakery, so I probably shouldn't have this much liquid while I'm out."

Jessica laughed. "Oh, I understand that. Hold on just a second, and I'll get down my shot glass." She hurried to the other side of the hut near the living room, grabbed something off the shelf, then hurried back to the kitchen. Washing the shot glass out in the sink, she ambled back over to the table, lifted my mug, and poured out some of my mushroom coffee. "Here you go." She handed Link the shot glass, then sat down across from me. "I hope you both enjoy."

"Smells good," Link said, holding the shot glass with both hands.

Knowing I had to take a sip before I could ask her any questions, I blew on the hot concoction, then took a tentative sip.

Being a cop meant you learned to school your features. And that's exactly what I did. Inside, I wanted to grimace, but on the outside, I knew my face gave nothing away.

"Unique," I said. "I definitely smell the mushrooms. It's very earthy."

Link chugged the entire glass, set it on the table, then patted his stomach. "Lovely! Absolutely delicious."

Jessica beamed. "Thank you. That means a lot."

I set the mug down and folded my hands on the table. "Jessica, we need to talk about Mya."

Jessica scowled and set her mug on the table as well. "What about her?"

"Have you not spoken to anyone in town today?" I asked.

"Yes. I mean, I was in town earlier today. I had to drop off some of my products. I spoke to several people in the café. Why?"

"About what time was that?"

"I'm not sure. I think I was at the café around eleven-thirty, maybe. My second cousin owns the café, and she buys at least six bags of my mushroom coffee and mushroom tea each week. To make sure it's fresh, I deliver three bags on Mondays and three bags on Thursdays."

I nodded. "So you were in town at the café today around eleven-thirty?"

Jessica picked up her mug and took a drink. "Yes. I know I was at the café before the noon rush. I dropped off my products, grabbed a piece of pie, and then left."

"What time did you leave?"

Jessica shrugged. "I don't know. Maybe around eleven-fifty. Like I said, the noon rush hadn't quite started, but there were a couple people coming in as I was leaving."

"Did you get a receipt?"

"My cousin doesn't charge me. I'm sorry, but what does all this have to do with Mya?"

I watched her carefully for a reaction. "Mya Harlan was murdered behind The Cozy Boutique around the lunch hour today."

Jessica's mouth dropped, and her eyes grew wide. "What? Mya is dead? Murdered? How?"

"The autopsy report hasn't come back yet, but evidence suggests it was an icepick to the throat."

Jessica yanked off her glasses, set them on the table, then rubbed her eyes. "I'm just in shock. I mean, I didn't like her at all, but I can't believe someone would actually kill her."

"Why didn't you like her?"

"Because she was a horrible person. We are—we were—" She paused and furrowed her brow. "I'm not sure what tense to use here. Anyway, it started way back in grammar school. I've always been the—well, kind of the weird one. You know what I mean?" She motioned to her wild hair. "Look at this hair. Mya used to tease me and call me 'wild witch' and get the other kids to tease me. Then Mya's dad died when we were in middle school, and things *really* got bad for me." She shrugged. "I think I was just an easy target for her. She was this beautiful polar bear shifter, and I was just this wild-looking winter hedge witch." She gestured around the room at the stack of crates. "It's what makes me ideal to grow different types of mushrooms. They need damp, cool weather with humidity." She wiggled her fingers. "I can do that as a winter witch."

I picked up my cup and pretended to take a sip. "Was she still bullying you all these years later?"

Jessica snorted and pushed back the sleeve of her sweater, revealing huge welts and bumps. "See these? Mya did this to me."

This time I knew my face registered surprise. "You're kidding me? How?"

Link zipped over to examine Jessica's arm. "Looks like an allergic reaction."

Jessica nodded. "It is. See, Mya was selling homemade lotions and soaps." She smoothed her sleeve back over her arm. "On Monday, Mya saw me in town at the café delivering my order. She stopped me outside and said she had something for me." She let out a small bark of laughter and looked away. "I don't know why I trusted anything she said. It's not a secret I'm allergic to tartrazine. Have been since birth." She glanced at me. "That's a yellow dye. It's often found in foods and products. I've always had to be careful."

"And Mya knew you were allergic?" I mused.

Jessica nodded. "Yes, Mya knew. She used to tease me about my allergy when we were kids." She tucked an errant curl behind her ear. "When she gave me the bottle of lotion Monday, I asked her if it had any tartrazine in it, and she assured me it didn't because she remembered I was allergic." A tear slipped down her cheek, and she brushed it away with her fingertips. "Well, as you can see, that wasn't at all true. I broke out in these horrible welts and blisters."

"I'm so sorry," I said.

Jessica snorted. "Oh, it gets better. When I called her to tell her what had happened, she laughed. She flat out laughed. She said she hoped my customers didn't hear about my leprosy, because I might lose all of my business. She said my customers might think the mushrooms will do the same to them." She shook her head. "I was terrified and angry. She did it on purpose."

I studied Jessica as I took another sip of the mushroom coffee. What she'd just revealed definitely put her at the top of my suspect list.

"I can understand why you'd be upset," I said. "Not only were you in physical discomfort, but she could have ruined your business."

Jessica threw up a hand. "Exactly."

Link cleared his throat. "Did you decide to take matters into your own hands, Jessica? Maybe wait until you saw her in town again and then take her out?"

Jessica shook her head, and her unruly curls bounced around her face. "No! I didn't do it."

"Okay," I said. "You told me you were in town from eleven-thirty until noon. Is that correct?"

"Yes, I guess it is. I left the café a little before noon, and then I came home. I only had that one delivery to make." She pointed to the crates against the wall. "Tomorrow, I'll do deliveries for three customers outside of town."

I nodded. "Did you ever see Mya Harlan in town today from eleven-thirty to twelve-thirty?"

"No."

"Did you see Brody Billings?" I asked.

Jessica's face registered surprise. "Mya's ex? No."

I furrowed my brow. "You didn't see him walking around town at all today during the noon hour?"

She shrugged. "I really didn't. I know Brody is angry at Mya. She left him holding the bag to a loan that is crippling him. Have you spoken to him yet about Mya's murder?"

"We did," Link said. "Do you know of anyone else who might have wanted Mya dead?"

Jessica shrugged. "Mya made a lot of people angry. You could throw a stone and hit someone she either owed money to or someone she angered. Oh, I know her old boss, Zelda Yarnell, was furious that Mya was selling her own version of beauty products. You might want to speak to her. In fact, I saw them arguing on the street outside the apothecary just last week. It looked heated."

Zelda Yarnell had told Link and me she hadn't spoken to Mya since she fired her last month.

"Thank you." I took another gulp of the lukewarm coffee and tried not to shudder. "If we have more questions, we know where to find you." I stood from the table. "Thank you for your time and for the mushroom coffee."

"Yes," Link said. "It was delicious."

10

"Something smells wonderful," Gwendolyn said as I shut the front door behind me.

We were later than expected, but I'd stopped by Amber Slater's house to rummage through Mya's bedroom after leaving Jessica's hut. I'd thought maybe *something* would jump out at me as a possible clue…but Mya's room had been sparse and sorely lacking in furniture and personal possessions.

"Bonnie's Burgers?" Gwendolyn asked.

I laughed. "Yep. How'd you know?"

"I know that smell." She flattened her hand against her growling stomach and laughed. "See! I already ate and my body still responds."

"The café was packed, and I didn't have a number to call ahead. So I asked a couple people on the street where another place to eat was."

"They steered you right." She sniffed the air. "Mushroom, grilled onion, swiss?"

Link chuckled. "For not being a werewolf, that's quite the sniffer you got there."

"I'm not usually a mushroom girl," I said, "but it just sounded good."

Gwendolyn glanced around the room before leaning in. "Probably because you went to see Jessica. Her mushrooms are amazing. Did you try her mushroom coffee? Fabulous, right?"

"I wanted another cup," Link admitted.

Was I the only one who wasn't blown away by mushroom coffee? And how did Gwendolyn know I visited Jessica today? Was the town *really* that small?

"Well," Gwendolyn said, "I won't keep you. I'm sure you're busy. Oh, the house gets a little drafty at night, and your room could get cold. I put an extra blanket on your bed. I hope that was okay?"

"That's fine. Thank you."

"No problem. And Savage was sound asleep when I went in." Gwendolyn clapped her hands together. "How about I send up a hot toddy in about an hour? Give your food time to digest? Would you like that?"

"I'd *love* that," I said honestly.

"Could I have a thimble of hot milk and honey?" Link asked.

"Of course. I'll bring it up in an hour."

Link and I said goodnight and headed up the stairs, burger and fries in hand. I was glad she'd ended the conversation because my mouth was watering just thinking about the juicy burger.

I unlocked the bedroom door and pushed it open. Savage looked up from his lounging position on my bed, then closed his eyes again. They immediately popped back open when he caught a whiff of the food.

"It's about time," he grumbled as he jumped off the bed. *"I*

practically starved today. Luckily, that kitchen witch came to check on me and brought me something."

I rolled my eyes. "I gave you something before we left. We've only been gone three hours."

"Three looooong hours."

"We could leave for three more," Link said. "See if that'll be the final nail in your coffin."

"Oh, vampire jokes. Supernatural humor. How amusing." Savage threaded himself between my feet. *"Enough with the small talk. What did you bring me to eat?"*

I sighed. It was a good thing Link and Savage didn't eat much, because now I was sharing my burger and fries with two others. I tossed the bag onto the desk.

"Give me a few minutes to get comfortable and call Lila real quick and make sure she'll be home tomorrow," I said. "Then I'll split the dinner."

Five minutes later, I was using a biodegradable knife to cut the cheeseburger into bite-sized pieces. After handing out the burger bites, I pulled out a couple fries each for Link and Savage.

"Do I get a drink?"

"I think the toilet seat's up," Link said.

I smiled and shoved a huge chunk of yummy burger in my mouth. No way was I wading into that dangerous discussion. It was usually best to ignore their bickering.

"So Lila knows we're coming tomorrow?" Link said as he nibbled on a tiny speck of hamburger.

"She knows," I said.

We ate the rest of our meal in silence. The only sound was the howling of wind and snow hitting the leaded windows.

"Did any of our suspects today jump out at you?" Link asked once our dinner was finished.

I shrugged. "They all had solid motives to want Mya dead."

My cell phone rang, and I smiled when I saw Rota's face pop up on the screen. "Hey, Rota. Perfect timing. I just finished dinner."

"Hello, Granddaughter. How was your day?"

"Good. Link and I questioned all but one of our persons of interest."

"Excellent. Want to give me their names so I can run background checks?"

"Sure. There's Amber Slater, Jessica Weston, Brody Billings, Zelda Yarnell, and Lila Vaughn."

"That's it?" Rota asked.

"I think so. I wasn't sure about the B&B owner, Gwendolyn Morrowson. She was the victim's latest employer, but when I spoke to Gwendolyn earlier today, she indicated she was at the B&B the entire time and that there was another couple here at the B&B as well. So right now, I don't consider Gwendolyn a suspect. Plus, she really doesn't have a motive to want Mya dead that I can ascertain."

"Okay," Rota said. "I'll run these names through the database and get back with you sometime tomorrow. How does that sound?"

"Sounds great. Thanks, Rota."

I disconnected and decided to video call Zane. I figured since I hadn't heard from him all day, he must still be somewhere in the arctic with no phone signal. To my surprise, his face appeared on the screen.

"Hey, Zane," I said. "I didn't think I'd get you."

He smiled, and my body instantly reacted. Zane was the kind of handsome that could turn a saint into a sinner.

"I'm not sure how long we'll have signal," he said. "I'm still in the middle of nowhere. How was your day?"

The screen scrambled, and Zane's face froze. I shook my

phone...not that it would do any good. It was just instinct. He finally unfroze, and I told him there had been a murder on Winter Island and that Link and I were on the case.

"I should be home by Sunday mid-morning," Zane said. "I can't wait to see—"

The screen went blank, and I cried out in frustration.

"Hope he wasn't eaten by a Yeti," Savage said as he licked his front paw. *"Or snowed under by an avalanche."*

I scowled at Savage. "Bite your tongue."

There was a knock at my door, and I rose to answer it. Gwendolyn stood on the other side, hot drinks and cookies on a tray.

"I brought you and Link your drinks," she said. "Plus, I added some cookies in case you needed a late-night snack."

Across the hall, a door opened, and the woman I'd spoken to earlier in the day stepped out into the hallway. "Hello. I hope it's not too much to ask, but could I get one of those, Gwendolyn? Anything warm to drink would be fine." She placed her hand on her stomach. "To be honest, my tummy has been a little upset all day. I came down around lunch to get an herbal tea, but I couldn't find you. Then we went out and had sweets from the tea shop and dinner tonight." She smiled self-consciously. "Well, I could use something soothing."

Gwendolyn frowned. "That's odd you couldn't find me earlier. Oh, I was probably in the greenhouse cutting fresh flowers for the table in the foyer. I try to change out the flowers every couple of days." Gwendolyn handed me the tray. "Here you go, Kara. And I'll bring you up an herbal tea as quickly as I can, Mrs. Fedderman."

I thanked Gwendolyn and shut the door gently with my shoulder.

"Are you thinking what I'm thinking?" Link asked.

"That I was once again overlooked and didn't get anything to drink?" Savage mused.

"Yep," I said, ignoring Savage. "Gwendolyn told us she was in the house the entire time during the lunch hour. Now she's saying she might have been out in the greenhouse." I set the tray down on the desk. "But what's her motive to kill Mya? No one today mentioned Gwendolyn when we asked who else might have wanted to hurt Mya."

Link nodded. "And it could be Gwendolyn really *was* in the greenhouse."

"I remember seeing flowers on the table next to the registry book." I picked up my hot toddy and blew across the top of the cup. "But maybe we should consider Gwendolyn a person of interest?"

"I don't think so," Savage said.

Link snorted and flew over to his espresso-sized cup of hot milk and honey. "And why is that, oh wise cat?"

"Because she came into the room today while you two were away. She could have snooped through your things, but didn't."

"What does that prove?" I asked.

Savage picked up his left front paw and started to groom himself again. *"That she's trustworthy. While you two were away, I went through everything, including what was in the bag Zahara had packed you. Why? Because I'm sneaky like that."*

I laughed. "I'm not sure if that's sound reasoning or not."

The window rattled as snow and wind blew against the glass. I shivered as a cold draft blanketed the room.

"Gwendolyn wasn't kidding," I said. "There *is* a draft in the house. Will you be okay, Link?"

He nodded and set his miniature cup on the desk. "I'll be just fine as long as you leave the bathroom light on. I can sleep on the soap tray under the light. Plenty of heat."

"That's great for the pixie," Savage said. *"But what about me? What if I freeze to death?"*

I snorted. "It won't get *that* cold. Plus, you have a ton of fur. You'll be fine."

"If I freeze to death overnight, I'm coming back to haunt you."

"I'll take my chances," I deadpanned.

11

"Everything looks wonderful," I said to Gwendolyn as I spread a thick layer of peanut butter onto my toast, then sat down at the dining room table across from Mr. and Mrs. Fedderman.

"Thank you. Just holler if you need anything else," Gwendolyn said before exiting the room.

"Is that all you're eating?" Mr. Fedderman asked. "Don't seem like it's enough to keep you going out in this weather."

"It's what she always eats," Link said as he shoved a fistful of muffin into his mouth.

"It's a light morning," I said. "I'll be working from here for a few hours."

"We heard about why you're here," Mrs. Fedderman said. "Such a terrible thing to happen."

"Did you know Mya?" I asked. "Had you spoken to her during your stay here?"

"Oh, yes," Mrs. Fedderman said. "The very morning she died."

"That would have been yesterday, Clauddie," Mr. Fedderman said gently.

Mrs. Fedderman laughed and slapped her husband playfully on the arm. "I know that, silly. Anyway, she dropped by our room to ask us if we had enough towels. She was leaving soon to go uptown, and she wanted to make sure we had everything we needed. I assured her we did, and that was the last time I spoke to her. Poor girl."

I finished my piece of peanut butter toast and washed it down with cinnamon-flavored coffee. "Did she seem upset? Or say anything else to you?"

Mrs. Fedderman shook her head. "No. In fact, she seemed happy. Well, happy for her." She leaned over the table conspiratorially. "We're here for the week, you see. And in the five days we've already been here, I'd spoken to her twice." She wrinkled her nose. "She wasn't what you'd call…hospitable. I guess that's the polite way to say it."

"But yesterday was different?" I asked.

Mrs. Fedderman nodded emphatically. "Oh, yes. She seemed excited about going uptown and delivering her soaps and lotions." She leaned back in her chair and picked up her coffee. "And she should have been. They were wonderful products. Smelled lovely and did great things for my skin."

"I wonder where she got the recipe?" I mused half to myself.

"Oh, she told me she used to work at the apothecary in town, and the owner shared the recipe with her."

My eyes met Link's across the table. Something told me there was no way Zelda Yarnell would knowingly share her recipes with Mya. I was already going to question Zelda about the last time she said she'd spoken with Mya…now it looked like I'd also be asking her about the possibility that Mya had stolen her recipes. Another motive for Zelda to want Mya dead.

I ate one more piece of peanut butter toast, then poured another cup of coffee and took it upstairs with me. Link had snatched a powdered sugar donut hole and was fluttering behind me as I strode up the steps, careful not to spill the coffee. Outside, the snow had slowed down, but the wind was still howling and beating against the windowpanes.

I pushed the bedroom door open, and Savage turned from the French doors and scowled. *"I suppose you'll make me go outside in this today?"*

"Not until later this afternoon," I said, setting down my coffee cup on the desk. "By then, it will probably die down."

"Die being the operative word here, I assume?"

I rolled my eyes. "You'll be fine. I'm only taking you with me when we travel to see Lila Vaughn."

"Are you at least going to feed me this morning?" Savage asked. *"I see the pixie is gorging himself."*

I turned and laughed. Link's face was covered in powdered sugar. He gave me a sheepish grin and went back to shoving the donut into his mouth. The donut hole was still larger than the size of his head.

"Gwendolyn gave me another can of cat food for you," I said. "Don't worry."

"I have to say, it's the best stuff I've ever eaten."

I frowned and stared down at the can. A skinny-necked black cat like the kind you'd sometimes see on the cover of paranormal mystery books stared up at me. "Really? You like this Tiki Cat better than the stuff I feed you?"

"A thousand times better."

I popped the top, then shuddered and winced as the smell permeated my nose. "It smells awful."

"It's delicious."

I frowned down at the can. "What are those huge balls?"

"*Quail eggs,*" Savage said, smacking his lips. "*Scrumptious.*"

I wrinkled my nose. "I'm not sure I'm comfortable with you eating that."

Savage narrowed his eyes and slowly sashayed over to me. "*Hand it over before someone gets hurt.*"

"Fine," I muttered, dumping the contents into the tiny bowl Gwendolyn had given me yesterday.

For a few seconds, the only sound in the room was Savage purring and scarfing up his food. Shaking my head, I tossed the can away and strode inside the bathroom to wash my hands.

As I walked back into the bedroom, movement outside caught my eye. Gwendolyn was in her greenhouse walking around. Could she really have just been outside yesterday when Mrs. Fedderman went looking for her? Was I reading too much into the fact Gwendolyn wasn't inside her house the entire hour?

My cell phone pinged with an incoming video.

"Hey, Rota," I said, smiling into the phone. "How are things in Mystic Cove?"

"Excellent. Alfred and I missed you and Link and Zane this morning during breakfast, but otherwise, things are fine here." She smiled into the phone. "Alfred is in the kitchen now pouring over peanut butter recipes. He's trying to find something special for your return."

My heart tripped over that declaration. Alfred had become important to me over the last few months. Almost like a father-figure. The fact he was now dating Rota just made it even more special.

"I can't wait to see and taste his creation," I said.

"I have background checks ready to go," Rota said. "You up for it?"

I glanced at Link and grinned. His face was still covered in powdered sugar, but at least the donut was almost gone. "I think we are. Let's get started."

12

I set the phone on the desk so Link and I could see and hear Rota. "Go ahead with your report."

"There's not a lot here," Rota said. "That's why I could get back to you so quickly."

I sighed. "And with Barbie still out of town, I won't get forensics back for another day or two. Hopefully, Doc Treestone will call with good news later today."

"First up is our victim, Mya Harlan," Rota said. "Polar bear shifter. Twenty-four. Single, no children. Criminal record consists of shoplifting in Mystic Cove, and then a terroristic threat against one of the suspects."

"Which suspect?" I asked.

"Jessica Weston. This happened about five years ago, but it's something to go on."

I nodded. "Jessica gave us the impression she'd been bullied by Mya since grade school."

"Mya had substantial debt, and the only employment I could find was a part-time job with Gwendolyn Morrowson at the

B&B. I did see where she had income coming in earlier in the year from Winter's Blend, an apothecary there on Winter Island. She currently rents where she's living."

"And she owes a couple months of back rent," I said.

Rota shook her head. "A financial disaster. Okay. First suspect is Amber Slater. Winter fairy. Forty-two. Born and raised on Winter Island. Divorced, no children. She's the owner of The Cozy Boutique. No criminal history, and the only thing in supernatural civil court was her divorce."

"Motive for Amber Slater," I said. "Mya was renting a room from her, but hadn't paid rent in over three months. Amber agreed to let Mya sell her beauty products in Amber's boutique to recoup money, but Mya had yet to pay Amber any profits. Amber was the person who found Mya dead behind The Cozy Boutique in the back alley."

"And Amber's alibi?" Rota asked.

"She was in her shop waiting for Mya to arrive," I said. "She had no customers because she'd closed for lunch, and so there's no one to corroborate she was in the boutique the entire time."

"I feel she's our weakest suspect," Link said. "I know she found the body, but that's really it for her. I realize she could have killed Mya because she owed her money, but it's not *that* much money yet."

I nodded. "Link's right. It's only about fifteen hundred dollars, and now, with Mya dead, Amber will never see a cent."

"Next up is Jessica Weston," Rota said. "Winter witch. Twenty-four. Single, no children. There's not a lot on Jessica. It's almost like she lives off the grid. No debt of any kind that I could see. Not even for a car or house."

"I'm not surprised," I said. "Her parents gave her the house when they moved away. It's the house she was born and raised in. I saw an old jalopy truck at her place, and I parked next to an old snowmobile when Link and I went to talk with her." I smiled. "And I'm sure she deals mostly in cash."

"But she has a motive," Link said. "When we talked with her, I could hear the anger and resentment in her voice when she spoke of Mya. There's a lot of pent-up rage there. And then when you take into consideration earlier this week, Mya intentionally gave Jessica something that would cause her to develop welts on her body, I can see Jessica having enough and killing Mya."

"I agree," I said. "Not only did Mya physically hurt Jessica, but then Mya threatened to tell all of Jessica's clients that the welts and rash were caused by Jessica's mushrooms, which would damage Jessica's mushroom business." I nodded. "Yeah, that's a powerful motive."

"Her alibi?" Rota asked.

"Jessica was in town during the time of the murder," I said. "She went to the café to deliver an order of mushroom coffee around eleven-thirty, ate a piece of pie, and left right before the noon rush hour for lunch. She said she went straight home and never saw Mya."

"Next, I have Brody Billings," Rota said. "Yeti. Twenty-nine. Single, no children. In debt up to his eyeballs. Two jobs on record, but neither is making him any money. I saw in his financials where he's stopped paying rent on the snowmobile shop, so I'm assuming he'll get an eviction notice soon. Criminal record of drunk and disorderly, public intoxication, and assault. I also found a civil suit filed here in supernatural civil courts. Looks like he was suing Mya."

I sat up at that announcement. "When did he do that?"

"Very recent. Filed five days ago."

"He didn't mention he'd filed a lawsuit against her when we spoke to him yesterday," I said. "He definitely has a motive to want Mya dead. Not only were they once engaged, but they took a joint loan out for thirty thousand dollars, and when Mya bailed on the relationship, she also bailed on the loan payment. That left Brody to pay back the entire thirty thousand. Every time Link and I have stopped by Brody's snowmobile rental shop, it's been empty. I don't think he does much business."

"His alibi?" Rota asked.

Link snorted. "We thought it was one big lie. Brody gave a ski lesson that lasted until eleven o'clock. It took him thirty minutes to get back to town. He went to his snowmobile shop, placed an order down the street at the café for lunch, but since it wouldn't be ready until twelve-fifteen, he went for a walk and return thirty minutes later. The thing is, when Kara asked him if he ever saw Mya walking in town, he said no. He never saw her."

"And you can't see that happening?" Rota asked.

I shook my head. "Not really. I mean, I *guess* it's possible he was walking on a street other than Main Street and just happened to miss Mya walking by, but it's weak. And like with Jessica Weston, there's a lot of deep-seated anger. Mya broke their engagement, and then stuck him with a thirty-thousand dollar debt. And I feel all of his answers have been cagey and half-truths."

"Next I have Zelda Yarnell," Rota said. "Winter witch. Forty-eight. Married, two grown children. Owns Winter's Blend. Criminal history shows a misdemeanor charge almost thirty years ago for trespassing and dancing naked."

I laughed. "Wait. That's a thing? I figured dancing naked under a full moon would be encouraged for witches."

"It was a citizen's arrest," Rota said. "She and three other girls jumped a fence on Winter Island and the landowner caught them."

I shuddered. "They were naked in the *snow?* Were they drunk?"

Rota laughed. "Doesn't say anything about public intoxication, so I'd say no."

"No way would you catch me dancing naked in the snow," I said. "I draw the line."

"And we're all thankful for that line," Savage said from his position atop my bed.

I scowled at him, then turned back to the phone. "Okay, so Zelda has a small criminal history. Anything else?"

"She and her husband have a little debt on the house they own, but nothing outstanding. The business is doing well, and the rent on the building is paid monthly."

"There's a lot of motive, though," Link said. "The first one being Zelda found out Mya was selling homemade beauty products and undercutting Zelda. Even the owner of the B&B here, Gwendolyn Morrowson, has been buying from Mya instead of Zelda. That meant Zelda was bound to lose big money soon."

"And Zelda's alibi?" Rota asked.

I glanced at Link. "Well, we just found out Zelda may have lied to us at least twice when we spoke to her yesterday. We are definitely talking with her later today to see if she changes her story."

"So, like Brody Billings, this Zelda woman has no problem lying," Rota said. "Yes, it sounds to me like you guys need to go back and talk with at least two of your suspects today." She grinned. "Shake the tree a little." She glanced down. "And now for our last suspect, Lila Vaughn. Winter fairy. Twenty-nine. Recently married, no children. Even using her maiden name, there wasn't any criminal history that popped for me. Financials for the last five years have been okay, but she recently married into money. Her husband's family owns a resort on Winter

Island. No debt on the resort. Lila recently filed a civil suit against Mya in the supernatural courts here in Mystic Cove."

"I haven't had an opportunity yet to question Lila," I said. "We are going this afternoon to do that. She lives about an hour away on the snowmobile. We know the motive for Lila to kill Mya, but we don't know her alibi yet."

"Well, that's all I've got for you," Rota said. "I hope that helped some."

"It did," I assured her. "We need to find out from Brody why he didn't mention he was suing Mya. He's been evasive this entire investigation."

"You two be careful out on that mountain," Rota said. "It can get dangerous over there on Winter Island."

"We'll be careful," Link promised.

I leaned in closer to the phone. "Did you get the coordinates and address for the Vaughn house?"

Rota rattled off the address.

"I'll call you tonight when we get back," I said before disconnecting.

13

"I can't believe we're taking Savage across the mountain with us," Link said as he took off his helmet and set it next to mine.

I grinned. "It'll be good for him to get out. Besides, the wind has died down, and the snow won't start back up until around four."

"We gotta be back by six so we don't get caught in the blizzard."

"I'm aware." I pulled open the door to the café and Link and I stepped inside.

The smell of breakfast food, grease, and coffee assaulted me. Even though it was after ten, there were still quite a few supernaturals sitting in booths, eating and drinking.

"I could go for a second breakfast, lass," Link said as he glided over to the counter. "Get something hot in me belly."

I rolled my eyes. "You just ate like an hour ago."

He grinned and waggled his pixie wings at me. "Aye. But that was an hour ago, lass."

"Can I help you?" a harried woman in a uniform of black pants and monogramed shirt asked as she whipped a pencil out of her hair.

I stepped up to the counter. "My name is Detective Hilder, and this is my partner, Link. Can we speak to the owner of the café?"

The woman studied us for a few seconds while she chewed her gum. She finally turned and yelled over her shoulder. "Janice, you got some people here needing to talk with you!"

A slight woman with brown spikey hair and almond-shaped blue eyes strode out from the kitchen area. I was fairly certain she was a winter fairy. When she saw us, she forced a smile and ambled over.

"I'm Janice Maythorn. How can I help you?"

I glanced over my shoulder as the bell over the door rang out. Two middle-aged werewolves lumbered inside, slamming the door behind them.

"Is there somewhere we could go for more privacy?" I asked.

"I got a booth available," Janice said. "Is that private enough?"

I nodded. "It'll do."

When we settled into the booth, I got right to the point. "Link and I need to ask you some questions about what happened yesterday."

"You mean about Mya Harlan getting murdered?"

"Yes," I said. "I spoke to your cousin, Jessica Weston, and she informed me she was here dropping off mushroom coffee for you around the lunch hour. Can you confirm this?"

"Jessica is my second cousin. And yes, she was here yesterday."

"What time, specifically?"

"I don't know. Probably around eleven-thirty or eleven-forty.

I know it was before the lunch rush because I remember thinking I hope she didn't stay long." She shrugged. "I know it sounds bad, but she was sitting in a booth, and I needed it for the crowd coming in. She dropped off the shiitake and oyster mushrooms I'd ordered, plus two bags of coffee and one bag of tea. She ordered a piece of pie, ate it, and then left." She leaned over the table. "My cousin didn't kill Mya Harlan."

I held up my hand. "I'm not here to accuse Jessica of killing Mya. I just needed to ask about her alibi."

Janice sighed. "Okay."

"So Jessica left the café right before the lunch rush," I said. "What about Brody Billings? Do you remember him coming in here yesterday for lunch?"

"Yes. But we were already serving people by then, and he placed a to-go order. If you want an exact time, I could check my receipts from yesterday."

"That would be great," I said. "Thank you."

She got up from the table, yelled at someone to bring us a couple pieces of pie while we waited, then hurried through a side door.

"I love this woman," Link said as he patted his stomach in anticipation of the pie coming our way.

By the time Janice returned, Link and I were half-way through our cinnamon apple pie a la mode.

"Good?" Janice mused.

"Delicious," I said.

"Amazing," Link agreed as he held an apple slice in front of his face with both hands.

"I found the receipt, and it says Brody paid for his lunch at twelve-thirteen." She slid the receipt across the table to me. "Does that help?"

"Sure does." I looked down at the receipt to double-check the time. "I think that's all we need."

"Enjoy your pie," she said. "It's on me."

As Janice got up from the table, I turned to Link. "If Brody got into town at eleven-thirty, but didn't pick up his lunch until twelve-fifteen, that gives him plenty of time to track down Mya, kill her, then pick up his lunch."

"I agree."

We sat in silence and finished our pie, then got up to leave. I was almost at the front door when someone grabbed hold of my hand. Looking down, I smiled at an elderly witch sitting in a booth with two other female witches her age.

"You the detective, dear?" she asked in a thin, warbled voice.

"I am. Can I help you with something?"

"More like we may be able to help you with something," one of the other women said. "Slide over Vida and let the girl sit."

The woman who'd grabbed my hand—Vida—slid down and patted the space next to her. Not seeing any other choice, I dropped down into the booth as Link landed on the table.

"I'm Viola, and this is my sister, Verna, and my other sister, Vida," the woman sitting across from me said. "We know you're looking into the murder of that polar bear she-devil shifter."

"Mya Harlan," I said.

Viola waved a wrinkled hand in the air. "Yes, yes. Anyway, we think you should know what we saw yesterday."

I arched an eyebrow. "What did you see?"

"Well," Viola said, "my sisters and I were sitting here minding our own business when we looked out the window and saw Zelda Yarnell run out of her apothecary, yelling and screaming at the woman who was murdered."

I frowned. This made *another* lie Zelda had told us yesterday. "What time was that, do you know?"

"It was eleven-fifty," Vida said. "I remember looking at my watch."

"So Zelda and Mya get into a screaming match," Viola said, "and then when it was done, Mya crosses the street and goes inside the bakery next door here. She comes out a few minutes later."

Vida waggled her finger. "With that silly pink coffee cup she always carried."

"And the basket," Verna said. "Don't forget about the basket."

Vida nodded. "Right. Mya always carried a coffee mug with her name on it, and so she had that and a basket with her." She leaned over until she was just a few inches from my face. "But that's not the scandalous part. The scandalous part came next. When Mya crossed the street and was in front of the apothecary window, she lifted the hand she was holding the coffee with and flipped Zelda the bird through the window! It was downright shameful."

The other two sisters tittered and shook their heads.

"Shameful," they echoed.

"What happened then?" I asked.

"Mya cut through the side alley and we lost sight of her," Vida said. "I'm not sure what happened to her after that."

"I'll tell you what happened," Viola said. "She went and got herself killed."

"So it was probably around twelve?" I asked. "When Mya left the bakery and flipped the bird through the apothecary window?"

The three witches nodded.

"That sounds about right," Vida said. "Was this helpful?"

I smiled and slid out of the booth. "Very helpful."

"Thank ye, lasses." Link winked as he fluttered his purple wings and lifted off the table. "Ye gave us a lot to think about."

The three elderly witches batted their eyelashes at Link and tittered some more as he wished them a good day.

"Don't let Lily see you flirting like that," I said as we stepped outside into the bright sun-kissed morning. "She might pluck out your wings."

Link laughed. "That she just might. So, what do you think?"

"I think Zelda lied to us yet *again*. But before we go talk with her, I want to step in here and check with the bakery. See if they can shed some light regarding the coffee. The cup in the alley was personalized. I wrongly assumed she brought it with her."

Link grinned. "You know what they say when you assume."

"Ha-ha. Hopefully, someone in the bakery can give me an exact time on when Mya bought the coffee."

14

I groaned as I stepped inside the bakery. Not only were the smells wonderful, but my eyes were immediately drawn to the display case and all the sugary goodness inside. Usually, I didn't crave sweets, but there was something about the combination of cold and snow that was making me want sugar and chocolate.

"Welcome to Snowy Sweet Bakery," the woman behind the counter called out.

As Link and I waited in line, the whispers and stares started. Ignoring them, I focused my attention on the display case, telling myself *not* to order anything. I'd already had a piece of pie and ice cream and it wasn't even eleven o'clock.

"Good morning," a perky, teenaged werewolf said. "How can I help you?"

"My name is Detective Hilder, and this is my partner, Link. Could I speak to a manager or the owner?"

"That would be me," the woman behind the cash register said. "Can you handle the front here, Charise?"

"Of course, Mrs. Lawton," the teenager said. "Take your time."

Mrs. Lawton motioned us to the back of the store, and I could feel all eyes on us. The woman pushed a curtain aside, and we followed her into a pristine kitchen complete with many modern conveniences.

"Is this about the murder?" Mrs. Lawton asked.

"It is," I said. "We've been told Mya Harlan stopped in yesterday just minutes before we believe she was killed. Can you tell me exactly what time she left here?"

"Of course. Give me a minute, please." Mrs. Lawton motioned for us to wait while she exited through another door.

"Maybe we should get a cookie or something for later," Link said. "You know, in case we need it while on the road crossing the mountain."

I grinned. "I can get behind that."

Mrs. Lawton wasn't gone but a few minutes before she hurried back into the kitchen. "I have it here. She paid for it with a card. I remember that. Receipt is timestamped for 11:56."

"Did you wait on her?" Link asked.

Mrs. Lawton glanced down at the receipt. "Yes. I made her a double white mocha in the travel mug she brought in, and then rang her up."

"So she brought the cup with her?" I mused.

Mrs. Lawton nodded. "Yes. It's a courtesy we offer to customers."

"How did she seem?" I asked. "How was her demeanor?"

"Well," Mrs. Lawton hedged. "I mean, most of us inside the store saw her arguing with Zelda Yarnell right before she came in for the coffee. When she came in, Mya seemed like she was in a good mood. Even smug."

I nodded. "Okay. Do you know of anyone who might have wanted Mya dead?"

"Besides Zelda Yarnell, you mean?"

"Yes," Link said. "Besides her."

Mrs. Lawton bit her lip and shrugged. "I mean, you hear rumors, you know? There's her ex-fiancé. He was pretty mad at her. The truth is, I try not to listen too much to gossip. I don't like it."

"Fair enough," I said. "Thank you for your time."

"Come back out with me, and I'll give you both something warm to take with you. It's cold out there, and you'll need all the sustenance you can get."

"If you insist," Link said, his wings glowing green. "I guess we can do that."

Link and I picked out a couple muffins and cookies, and then left the shop. Once we were a few stores away, I glanced up at Link hovering near my shoulder.

"So we know Mya buys a coffee roughly five minutes before noon," I said, "and by twelve-fifteen, her dead body is discovered in the alley behind the boutique by Amber Slater."

"That's a very narrow window, Kara."

I nodded. "It is. And if we think about our suspects, we know Brody, Zelda, and Jessica all had to have seen her. The three of them were within this general area."

"For all we know, Lila Vaughn could be in this mix as well."

"Something's gotta give," I said. "Let's see if we can't push Zelda or Brody into telling us why they both lied to us."

As I walked by my snowmobile, I lifted the seat and shoved the bag of muffins and cookies in the storage area before crossing the street and strolling to the apothecary. Before opening the door, I peeked inside and saw Zelda using magic to move items around the store.

I opened the door and Link and I entered the shop.

"Good morning. Welcome to…" Zelda's voice trailed off when she caught sight of us.

"Good morning," I said. "I think we need to have a little talk."

Zelda lowered her hands, and the products dropped back down onto the shelves. "What about, Detective?"

I walked closer to the counter. "After speaking with several witnesses, it seems you may have inadvertently left out some vital information."

"That's her way of letting you save face," Link said.

Zelda scowled. "What kind of vital information?"

"You want me to spell it out for you?" I mused. "How about the fact you lied about not seeing Mya yesterday? You told us you hadn't seen or spoken to her in over a month. Yet, we have eyewitnesses who say they saw you and Mya arguing in front of the apothecary yesterday, a little before noon. Care to explain?"

Zelda flexed her jaw, her face red with anger. "What did you expect me to say? That I stopped Mya, and we had an argument on the sidewalk just minutes before her body was discovered in my back alley a couple doors down? Do you know how that would have looked? It would've looked like I killed her. And I didn't."

"I'll tell you how it looks," Link said. "It looks like you don't have a problem lying to law enforcement."

"He's right," I said. "So are you changing your statement today? Can you tell me when the last time you spoke to Mya Harlan was?"

Zelda huffed and crossed her arms. "Okay, it was around lunchtime. Your witness was probably right. I saw her walk in front of my window, and I ran outside to stop her. She was carrying a basket, and I wanted to know what was inside. I just *knew* she was making a delivery to The Cozy Boutique."

"And was she?" I asked.

"I guess so. She had *my* products inside." She gave a bitter snort. "I mean, the bottles had a fancy label on them, but it was *my* product."

I nodded. "Which brings me to another question. Do you believe Mya stole your recipes and passed them off as her own?"

Zelda pursed her lips and narrowed her eyes. "That's *exactly* what I think happened. I make all the products. I hired Mya to stock shelves and run the cash register. A while back, I caught her in the storage closet where I make all my products. I asked her what she was doing, and she said the door was open, and so she was just going to close it, but decided to take a peek inside. She said she was curious. I knew for a *fact* there was no way I left the door opened." She sighed. "I didn't give it any thought until I started getting calls from store owners in town, wanting to know if I was aware Mya was trying to sell her own beauty supplies to them." She shook her head. "That's when I remembered a few months ago finding her in my workroom."

"Let's go back to the argument on the sidewalk yesterday around lunchtime," I said. "After you two argued, where did you go? And where did she go?"

"She went across the street to the bakery, and I went inside my store."

"Did you see Mya exit the bakery a few minutes later?" I asked.

"No."

I crossed my arms over my chest. "So you never saw Mya walk back across the street, look through your window, and flip you the bird?"

"I did not."

"Did you see her cut down the side alley of your store?" I asked.

"I did not." She threw one hand in the air. "Listen, if it wasn't Brody who killed her, then it had to be Lila Vaughn. She came in here the day I fired Mya, and she was spitting mad. She was threatening to sue Mya."

"One last question," I said. "Did you ever see Jessica Weston come out of the café yesterday?"

"Jessica?" Zelda glanced up at the ceiling, her brow furrowed. "Actually," she said, looking back at me, "now that you asked that, I think I did. I didn't think anything about it at the time. I was more focused on Mya. But I think as Mya entered the bakery, Jessica exited the café next door."

I nodded. "Did the two women see each other or speak to each other?"

Zelda shook her head. "Oh, no. Jessica did what she always does and tried to make herself invisible. I guess that's why I didn't think anything about it. Jessica turned her face and all but ran in the opposite direction down the sidewalk. I have no idea where she ran off to."

"I think that's everything," I said. "But if we come back with more questions, you better be forthcoming, Zelda. It does no good to hide the truth from Link and me. We *will* discover what happened to Mya Harlan." I gave her a tight smile. "Have a good day."

I shut the front door and stepped out into spitting snow, Link hovering near my shoulder.

"Seems no one wants to tell us the truth in this investigation," he said.

"Looks that way," I agreed.

Link grinned and patted his hip. "My sword has a way of making people talk."

I snorted. "Let's hope it doesn't come to that."

My cell phone rang, and I was happy to see Doc Treestone's face pop up on my screen. Sliding my finger across the icon, I answered the call. By the time he finished talking, I was once again frustrated. We disconnected, and I shoved the phone back in my pocket.

"Not good?" Link asked.

"Not helpful," I said. "From everything we've discovered this morning, we basically knew the time of death already. Mya left the bakery carrying a coffee and basket of goodies at 11:56. Fifteen minutes later, her body would be discovered. Outside of the two puncture wounds in Mya's neck from the ice pick, there's nothing else about the murder that stands out. Doc Treestone said the tox report came back clean." I sighed. "I really need Barbie to get back soon so she can analyze Mya's jacket. That might point us in a better direction."

"She should be back in the morning, and even though it's a Saturday, I'm sure she'll come into the lab when she hears there's been a murder and there's evidence to analyze."

"I hope you're right," I said.

The door to the bakery across the street opened, and Brody Billings strode outside.

"Perfect timing," I said. "Let's go see if we can press his buttons."

15

"Brody Billings," I called out, lifting my hand in the air. "Wait up, please."

Brody glanced across the street at us, and I swear I could hear his groan from where I stood. Looking both ways, I jogged across the street and carefully stepped up onto the snowy sidewalk.

"Detective Hilder. Link. You both are still here, huh?" he asked, blowing on the liquid in his to-go cup.

"Until we solve this case," I said. "Can I ask you a couple questions?"

He lowered his cup and frowned. "I can't exactly say no, right?"

I smiled. "Right. Is it true you recently filed a lawsuit against Mya with the paranormal civil court in Mystic Cove?"

"It is. Did I forget to mention that yesterday?"

This time my smile was more a smirk. "Yes, you did."

Brody shrugged. "Must have slipped my mind in my grief. Sorry about that, Detective."

"I'm sure you are," Link growled as he hovered between Brody and me.

Brody's eyes flickered to Link before focusing back on me. "Was there anything else? I need to open my store. My morning ski lesson cancelled today, so I came to town earlier than normal." He lifted his cup in the air. "I stopped by here to get some caffeine before heading to open my shop. Which reminds me. Is the snowmobile still working out for you?"

"It is, thanks."

A gust of wind blew by me, nearly knocking me off my feet. I staggered before righting myself. Link wasn't as fortunate, and he tumbled backward in the air.

Brody lifted a hand and whispered a spell that caused Link to halt mid-flip.

"You okay, Link?" I asked.

Patting down his puffy jacket, he flipped back up and nodded. "I think so." He zipped back over to where we stood. "You can wield magic?"

Brody nodded. "A little bit. Got some witch ancestry in me, and it's always come easily enough."

Link looked up at the sky. "We better get a move on if we're going to the northeast side of the island, Kara. It looks like it could start storming before the normal six o'clock time."

Brody frowned. "Yeah, it is." He moved his head toward the bakery. "Word inside is there's an ice storm heading our way in the next hour or two. You shouldn't be driving anywhere right now. It's not safe."

"Thank you for your concern," I said, "but we still have interviews to conduct."

Brody shook his head. "If you mean you need to go talk to Lila Vaughn, I'm telling you right now you might want to reconsider. It's an hour on good days." He gestured to the sky. "This isn't a good day. It'll probably take you over an hour and a half with the ice."

"Then I guess we better go now," I said. "Have a good day, Mr. Billings."

I turned and walked the short distance to the snowmobile. After donning our helmets, Link slipped down inside my coat. I looked over at the bakery and froze when I realized Brody Billings was still standing there…silently watching me.

With one last wave, I turned on the machine and slowly pulled out onto the snow-packed street. If I didn't see snow again for a year, that would be just fine with me. I couldn't imagine having to live day in and day out in the dismal conditions.

It didn't take but a few minutes to reach Snow Haven B&B. As Link and I headed for the front door, it opened and Gwendolyn stood in the doorway.

"Word just came in over the radio that a slow-moving ice storm is headed toward the south side of the island." She stepped back to let us inside. "You might want to stay inside the rest of the day."

"Can't," I said. "We still have two more people to speak to."

Gwendolyn bit her lip. "Then can I at least give you a thermos of chicken noodle soup and a thermos of coffee to take with you?"

"That would be great," I said. "Thanks, Gwendolyn."

"Okay. When are you heading back out?"

"I just stopped by to get Savage," I said.

Gwendolyn gasped. "Are you sure you want to take him out in this weather?"

"We could leave him behind," Link said.

I narrowed my eyes at Link. "I'd feel better if he came with me."

"I have a small-animal coat that should fit him," Gwendolyn

said. "You're welcome to put him in it. I also have a blanket you can take with you."

"You're a lifesaver, Gwendolyn," I said. "We'll be back down in about ten minutes."

Savage was napping on the bed when I opened the door to my bedroom. Or, at least, he was pretending to nap. By the way his ear twitched when I walked inside the room, I knew he was faking it.

"I know you're awake," I said. "I need to use the restroom, then we can head out." I glanced at Link. "I think we should go question Jessica real quick about her encounter on the street yesterday with Mya."

"I agree," Link said.

"Do I have to go?" Savage whined as he opened one eye. *"You know if I don't get in a solid eighteen hours of sleep time, I get cranky."*

I rolled my eyes. "You're going."

"Do I have to wear that humiliating helmet?" Savage asked as he leaped off the bed.

"Yes. Oh, I also have a cat coat you can wear so you don't get cold."

"Oh, the hits just keep rolling in."

Link laughed. "You might like a little adventure."

Savage yawned, giving me a view of the inside of his mouth —sharp teeth and all. *"Do I look like a cat who enjoys adventure?"*

16

"I've never been so humiliated in all my life," Savage said. "And I have nine lives to pull from!"

I laughed and yanked my helmet off my head as Link flew out of my coat pocket. Reaching over, I loosened Savage's strap on his helmet.

"I mean, seriously! Look at this jacket! It's bedazzled!"

"It's cute," I said. "And I didn't know when I said yes to the coat that it was a sparkle coat. Just be glad it's something to keep you warm."

Savage looked down at the pink and purple rhinestone-encrusted coat. "I think I'd rather freeze to death at this point."

"I vote for that," Link joked.

To be fair, the coat *was* a little over-the-top. Every time we hit the sun just right, my handlebars shimmered from the glare of Savage's jacket. And that was with my back to him. Goodness only knew what would happen to my eyes if he were sitting in front of me.

"Knock it off, you two," I said. "I can't have you guys making me laugh while questioning a suspect."

The three of us made our way up the slippery cobblestone walkway of Jessica Weston's hut. I did my best not to giggle at Savage's pink and purple rhinestone coat...but I wasn't successful.

He must have known I was laughing at him because he whipped his head around and glared. *"Don't forget I know where you sleep at night, Valkyrie."*

I raised my gloved hand and knocked on the door. A few seconds later, Jessica called from inside the house, asking us to hold on.

The door finally swung open, and she frowned. "Yes?"

"Jessica, we need to talk with you again for a few minutes. Is now a good time?"

Jessica glanced out over my shoulder at the sky. "I have some supplies I still need to deliver, and I heard it's going to get icy soon. Can we do this another time? Or can you promise to be quick?"

"I'll be quick," I said.

She sighed and opened the door wider. "Then c'mon in." She glanced down at Savage and clapped her hands. "Oh, look at you! Aren't you just the cutest little kitty in your sparkly jacket? What's her name?"

Link laughed, and Savage hissed.

"Savage. And he's a boy," I said. "I didn't have a jacket for him, but Gwendolyn Morrowson was kind enough to let me borrow one she had."

Jessica's hands flew to her cheeks. "Oh, I'm sorry. I just assumed. Please, forgive me."

"You are all dead to me," Savage said as he sashayed inside the hut, head and tail held high.

Eight crates were stacked near the door, each one piled high with various mushrooms. Next to the crates were two baskets filled with what looked like gray powder inside glass jars.

I turned to face Jessica. "We've had an eyewitness tell us they saw you exit the café yesterday at the same time Mya entered the bakery next door. Do you remember that?"

"No."

I arched an eyebrow. "You don't remember seeing Mya on the sidewalk around noon? She would have been about six feet from you. Anything ringing a bell?"

Jessica sighed. "Okay, maybe I noticed her. But I didn't say anything to her." She held up her hands. "What do you want from me? I already told you I did everything I could to stay away from her. If I saw her on the street, I always went the other way. So, yes. Maybe I remember seeing her enter the bakery as I was leaving the café. But I didn't stop her and engage in a conversation. I didn't even say hi to her. So what does it matter if I saw her on the sidewalk?"

"She's a slippery one," Savage said. *"I'm going with she's the guilty person. Arrest her so we can get off this freezing iceberg island."*

"It matters because I asked if you saw Mya at all yesterday," I said, "and you said no."

"I didn't see or talk with her. Not really." She crossed her arms over her chest. "I know for a fact you have better suspects than me. I called Brody Billings last night to see how he was holding up, and he's an absolute mess. He also told me you know about Lila Vaughn and how she was suing Mya. Then a mushroom customer called me to place an order last night, and we got to talking. She said she heard you were in the apothecary talking to Zelda Yarnell. So I know for a fact there are tons of other suspects out there who had it out for Mya Harlan. More than just me, I mean." She glanced out the window, then cut her eyes back to me. "Did you talk to Lila yet?"

"We're heading to talk to Lila after we leave here," I said.

Jessica's eyes went wide. "Now? Are you sure that's wise? I mean, I'm making deliveries outside of town, but only a couple, so the roads should be okay for a while yet. But you're talking about going over the mountain. I'm not sure you should do that."

"Listen to the crazy killer," Savage said. *"We should go back to the B&B, have a delicious meal of tuna and salmon, and then sleep in front of the fireplace."*

"If it gets too bad, I'll turn around and wait until tomorrow," I lied.

Jessica nodded. "Okay. Look, I need to make my deliveries before the ice blows in."

"We'll leave you to it," I said.

"Oh, hey," Jessica said. "Is it true? Brody told me you're dating Zane, the fallen angel."

I bit back a smile at the hero worship I heard in her voice. "Yes, I am. He's also my usual partner, but he's on assignment elsewhere right now."

"I've never met him, but I've heard stories." She pushed her glasses up her nose. "I hope it was okay Brody told me."

Link chuckled. "'Tis no secret, lass."

Jessica nodded and tucked a wild curl behind her ear. "Cool. Well, I really need to go. I have quite a few deliveries, and I don't want to get caught out in the storm."

"Be careful," I said.

"Same to you," Jessica replied.

17

It took an hour and thirty-five minutes to cross the mountain. While treacherous and exhausting, it was worth it. More than once, I wanted to stop and just observe the beautiful nature around me. The glistening snow-capped mountains, frosted pine forests, icy rivers, and frozen waterfalls. But I knew if I wanted to get back to the B&B before the blizzard hit, I had to keep moving.

When I finally made it to the Vaughn house, I had to check the address twice. This wasn't a simple little home in the mountains…it was a mini ice castle!

An honest-to-goodness mini ice castle.

"We're here," I said, pulling off my helmet and giving my hair a good shake.

"You're gonna need to do more than that," Savage grumbled as he hopped down off the back of the snowmobile and did a slow stretch. *"Your hair is hideous."*

"Want me to fluff it up with my wing wind?" Link asked as he zipped quickly back and forth in front of me.

I laughed and ran my hands through my hair. "No, it's okay."

"It's not okay. It's hideous."

I stood, opened the storage container on the snowmobile, unzipped the backpack Gwendolyn had given me when we left, and rummaged around inside. There were two thermoses, cookies, the muffins from the bakery, and a couple protein bars. At the bottom of the bag was a hair tie I'd thrown in at the last minute. Bending over, I gather my hair, flipped back up, then wound it into a bun and secure it. "All done."

Savage yawned. *"It's passable."*

The air was frigid and bleak, and I could see my breath as we trudged to the front door. The crunch of the hard snow beneath my boots was the only sound I could hear. The Vaughns were totally isolated on this side of the mountain.

"I've never seen anything like this before," Link admitted as he hovered near my shoulder.

"Me neither," I said.

The castle was no bigger than three thousand square feet, but it was still impressive. The exterior of the ice castle was carved from massive ice blocks. There were two towering turrets, one on each side of the castle, and a thick layer of frost covered the ice, making it sparkle like diamonds.

I glanced down at Savage. "The castle walls look like your coat."

"Ha-ha," he said dryly. *"Good one."*

I knocked on the double door made entirely of ice, and then reached down and rang the doorbell. A few minutes later, it was opened by the handsome blue-eyed polar bear shifter I'd seen in Brody's store yesterday.

"We meet again," he said. "I assume you're the detective who wants to speak to my wife?"

"I am. I'm Detective Hilder, and this is my partner, Link. And my cat, Savage."

"Bruno!" a female voice called out. "Is it the detective?"

"Yes, Lila," the polar bear shifter hollered back before turning to me. "Please come in."

I stepped into the foyer and marveled at the beautiful interior. A Cathedral ceiling framed by ice pillars drew my eye to an elegant *Gone with the Wind* snow-packed grand staircase. Just in the entryway alone, there were three ice chandeliers.

"I wondered about the flooring," I murmured.

"Snow-packed," Bruno said.

I smiled. "I was afraid it would be ice."

"Welcome to Glacier Castle," a beautiful blonde-hair woman said as she glided into the foyer. She was dressed in gray wool pants and a cream sweater. "I'm Lila Vaughn. And I assume you've met Bruno?" She wrapped both arms around Bruno's arm and smiled up at him. "My adoring husband."

"I have. And this is my partner Link. And my cat Savage."

"Savage?" she asked, taking in the pink sparkle jacket. "Boy or girl?"

"Can I please scratch her eyes out?" Savage asked.

"Boy," I said.

"Oh, isn't he adorable?" Lila said. "And all bundled up in that glorious pink and purple shimmer coat." She clasped her hands together. "Too cute."

"I feel the sudden urge to yack in one of her shoes."

"Well, come in," Lila said. "You must be exhausted after that long trek. Did you drive or take a snowmobile?"

"Snowmobile," I said.

Link flew over and hovered near my shoulder. "You're a long way from town."

"We are," Lila agreed. "But Bruno's family owns the resort

on the mountain, so he only has to travel to the resort for work, and I work from home." She smiled. "Let's go sit in the living room, shall we?"

Link, Savage, and I followed Bruno and Lila down a wide hallway and into a spacious living area with ice sofas and ice chairs. Gray and black faux pelts and blankets were strewn about the ice-sculpted furniture. Even the coffee and end tables were made from blocks of ice.

I sat down on one of the ice sofas, Savage and Link flanking me. It was surprisingly warm. "Can I ask? Is your entire house made from ice? Even your shower and kitchen?"

Bruno smiled and shook his head. "No. I built this place about ten years ago. I was living at the resort my parents owned, but I wanted my independence. A place to call my own." He waved his hand in the air. "It's a little over-indulgent, I know, but it works for me." He patted Lila's knees. "For us."

I schooled my face so I wouldn't show my emotion. Bruno had a way of talking that made him seem both arrogant and placating. Like if he didn't talk to me in a slow, haughty tone, I might not understand him.

"Anyway," he continued, "I hired an elemental fire witch from Mystic Cove to spell the stove and bathrooms to always be warm without melting the floor or surrounding area." He chuckled. "Conveniences of magic."

"But everything else is made of ice," Lila interjected. "The beds, shelves, all of it." She leaned forward in her ice chair. "Can I offer you all something to drink?" She motioned to a bar on the far side of the room. It, too, was made entirely of ice. "We have cocktails if you need to warm up."

"No, thanks," I said. "I stopped when we crested the mountain, and we all had some hot coffee."

Bruno sat back in his seat and crossed his legs. "Then let's get on with this unpleasantness, shall we?"

"Of course," I said. "You are both aware Mya Harlan was murdered yesterday in town?"

"We are," Lila said.

"Time of death was between twelve and twelve-fifteen," I said. "Lila, how did you know Mya?"

"We went to school together," Lila said. "We weren't in the same class or anything, but we knew of each other."

"How would you describe your relationship?" I asked. "Were you friendly? Rarely spoke?"

Lila shrugged. "I guess up until a couple months ago we were acquaintances."

"Then what happened?" I asked.

Lila turned and looked adoringly at Bruno. "So about four months ago, Bruno and I were married. I was in the apothecary one day about two weeks before the wedding, looking for bridesmaid gifts, and Mya was in there working. She pulled me aside and told me she could do a basket for each bridesmaid for less than what I would spend in the apothecary. So I told her that sounded great. I gave her the money upfront for eleven baskets—one for each bridesmaid."

"You had eleven bridesmaids?" I mused.

"'Tis nothing," Link said. "One of my nieces just got married last year, and she had twenty-three bridesmaids. Her husband came from a large pixie family like us. Large weddings are not uncommon among supernaturals."

"That's true," Lila said. "Although, nothing is as over-the-top as werewolf weddings." Lila rolled her eyes. "*Everyone* has to be in the wedding party or it can turn into a brawl."

"Okay," I said. "Back to Mya. How much did you pay her to make the eleven baskets?"

Lila crossed her arms over the chest. "Twenty-five hundred dollars. But the money wasn't the issue. I took umbrage with the fact she took my money, then ghosted me. Every time I'd try to call her, she would let it go to voicemail. Then, when I finally *did* track her down, she gave me some ridiculous excuse and promised she'd have it to me before the wedding, but it never happened. I had to scramble and buy my girls something else. It was humiliating." She pursed her lips. "Then I find out after we're married that Bruno had given his cousin and Mya thirty thousand dollars to open that ridiculous snowmobile store in town. Granted, this all happened before we were married, but still! It's the principal of the matter. Especially when you take into consideration that Mya took my money for the bridesmaids' baskets and never delivered."

"You didn't know about the loan?" I asked.

Lila waved a hand in the air. "No, of course not. I rarely bother with knowing all of Bruno's dealings, so it didn't surprise me. It just…"

When she didn't finish, I prompted her. "It just upset you?"

"Of course it upset me!" Lila exclaimed.

Bruno placed his hand on Lila's knee. "What my wife is trying to say is that while she was upset, she didn't kill Mya."

"Right," Lila said. "I didn't murder Mya."

"When was the last time you saw or spoke to Mya?" I asked.

"When I filed the lawsuit against her last month," Lila said. "I called her to let her know she was going to be served. That was the last time."

"Did you go into town yesterday?" Link asked.

Lila shook her head. "No. I worked from home all day."

I glanced at Bruno. "And you? Were you in town yesterday?"

Lila laughed. "I can promise you he wasn't. I have to *beg*

Bruno to take the day off from work. He's married to his job." She pouted. "But hopefully that will change soon."

I arched an eyebrow at Bruno. "So you *weren't* in town yesterday?"

"I think you know I was," Bruno said.

Lila's head and body whipped around to face Bruno. "What? You were in town yesterday? Why?"

Bruno arched an eyebrow at his wife. "I went to talk to my financial advisor, and then I stopped by to talk with Brody about the loan payment. You've been hounding me nonstop to do something about it. Or have you forgotten?"

Lila's face flushed. "Of course I haven't forgotten. But you didn't say anything to me about talking to Brody." Her eyes darted to me. "Or talking to Mya."

"Because I didn't talk to Mya," Bruno said. "I spoke to Brody around two o'clock. If the rumors are true, Mya had been dead for over an hour by then."

That statement hung awkwardly in the air.

Was I on the wrong track? Maybe it wasn't Lila who'd murdered Mya, but Bruno? He was getting hounded by his new wife to do something about the loan he'd given Brody and Mya, *and* he knew Mya had taken his new bride for over two thousand dollars.

"Mr. Vaughn," I said, "can you tell me where you were yesterday between eleven-thirty and twelve-thirty?"

"Of course." He brushed his hand across his knee as though he were brushing lint off his trousers. "I was at the resort until eleven-thirty. I left and headed into town. I met with my financial advisor at Blue Sage restaurant for a working lunch around twelve-thirty. Even though you haven't asked, I'll also volunteer that after the luncheon, I went to visit my grandmother who lives in town for about an hour before going to see Brody. It was while

I was at my grandmother's house that I heard the unfortunate news about Mya."

"You say you left the resort around eleven-thirty," I said. "Did you speak to anyone? Tell anyone you were leaving?"

"No. I am my own boss."

I lifted one hand in the air. "So no one can corroborate you left around eleven-thirty?"

A muscle jumped in Bruno's jaw, and he narrowed his blue eyes at me. "No. I believe the last person I spoke to was my office manager around eleven-fifteen. I wanted to know if she'd seen Brody anywhere. His last ski lesson ended at eleven, and I'd searched everywhere for him."

I knew that was probably true. Brody had told me he all but bolted from the mountain at eleven, so he wouldn't run into his cousin.

"What time did you get to town?" I asked.

Bruno shrugged. "I don't know. Probably around twelve."

"But your lunch appointment wasn't until twelve-thirty?" Link asked.

He sighed. "That's right. I sat in my car and did some work before I went inside the restaurant around twelve-twenty."

"So," Link said, "you're telling us the last time you spoke to anyone before heading to town yesterday was eleven-fifteen, and even though you arrived in town around noon, you didn't go inside the restaurant until twelve-twenty?"

"I know what you're implying," Bruno said. "Here's the problem with the whole motive thing." He lifted both hands in the air. "I don't have one. Look around you. I obviously have money. Why would I kill some woman I don't even know for a few thousand dollars?"

"Technically," I said, "it was more than a few thousand dollars, wasn't it? You had your wife angry at you over Mya's deceit, and you had your cousin unable to pay the thirty thousand he and Mya had borrowed from you." I shrugged. "That might be a motive, wouldn't you agree?"

"He looks like he's swallowed a lemon," Savage said.

"I wouldn't kill someone over money," Bruno said tightly.

"One last question," I said. "While we were in Brody's store yesterday, I heard you tell Brody he didn't want you to take the next step. What did you mean by that?"

Bruno let out a bark of laughter. "Are you thinking I meant I would kill him like I killed Mya? Because you are way off base. I simply meant I'd go through legal channels to collect my money."

"Of course you did." I stood and smiled at the couple. "Thank you for your time."

18

"Why're we stopping?" Link asked as he popped out of my coat pocket. "We stopped once about forty minutes ago, and we've barely crossed the halfway point. We still have a good thirty miles before we get to town."

"I know." I said, yanking off my helmet. "But I thought we'd stop and have a muffin. Plus, maneuvering in this icy sleet is a lot more difficult than I thought it would be."

"I could go for another bite," Savage said from his position behind me on the snowmobile's seat.

I'd stopped on a frozen lake with nothing but ice for miles around. To the right of the snowmobile was the base of the mountain. We'd just finished the most treacherous part of the journey, and I needed to rest a moment.

I still had on the waterproof backpack from our last stop, so Link unzipped the bag and rummaged around inside. "We'll eat the muffins, but we need to get back on the road soon before the blizzard really hits, Kara. This icy rain is awful, but when you mix in the snow that's due soon, it's going to be impossible to get around in." He handed me a muffin, then looked up into the sky. "Looks like it could come any..." His voice trailed off.

"What? What's wrong?" I asked, giving Savage a corner of the muffin.

"Magic!" Link cried. "Duck!"

I didn't even have time to throw up a protection spell before the wave of magic hit. The surge sent me reeling backward, and I cried out as I fell onto the hard ice. Before I could get back up...I heard the crack under me!

The snowmobile and I both plunged into the icy, frozen water at the same time. I tried to scream and reach for Savage before I went underwater...but Link was faster. He swooped in, wings buzzing erratically, and grabbed Savage by the shoulders of his bedazzled coat.

That was all I saw before the churning black water pulled me under. Panic filled my body as I tried desperately to claw my way to the top, terrified of drowning. It wasn't until I felt a change in the water around me that I remembered I could shift into a mermaid thanks to Queen Atla.

I forced myself to relax, open my eyes, and assess my situation. The snowmobile was slowly sinking to the bottom of the lake, but I seemed to be okay. I flipped my fin and pushed toward the top of the water. When my head broke the surface, I instinctively gasped for air.

"Kara!" Link cried out. "You okay, lass?"

I glanced up and saw Link hovering above me, Savage dangling precariously in the air from Link's hands. I shook my head to clear it.

"I demand to be put down immediately!" Savage hissed. "This is so humiliating!"

"I saved your life, Beast," Link said.

"Are we still being hit?" I asked.

"No. I think the coward ran after they threw the magic wave." Link flew closer to me, causing Savage to scream in terror. "Oh, hush. I ain't gonna drop you. Can you get out on your own, Kara?"

"I think so."

I could feel the weight of the backpack pulling me down, which was comforting. At least the food and coffee hadn't been lost. Unlike the snowmobile. I grabbed onto the edge of the thick ice and hauled myself out of the water. The minute my lower half hit the cold air, my fin gave way to legs. Standing up, I lifted my hands in defense of whatever attack might come our way.

But nothing happened.

Dropping my hands, I sighed. "We lost our ride. And our phone. It was in the storage seat on the snowmobile. Guess we walk into town from here?"

I glanced down at my clothes and gloves, thankful for the magic that allowed me to get out of a body of water and still remain dry. At least I didn't have to worry about catching pneumonia and dying. I'd need to thank Queen Atla again the next time I saw her.

"No," Link said. "We can't walk from here. It's too dangerous. We need to take cover. There's no way we can make it to town now before the blizzard hits. We were still thirty minutes away on a snowmobile. We'd never survive if we walked."

"We're gonna die out here," Savage whined. *"I lost my blanket in the water. I'll freeze to death now."*

"We aren't gonna die," I said, reaching up to grab Savage away from Link. "Thanks for saving Savage, Link."

"It was me pleasure, lass."

"What do you say, Savage?" I said, setting him down on the ice.

"The next time you grab me, be more gentle."

"Savage," I warned.

He flicked his tail and sighed. *"Fine. Thank you for not letting me plunge into the icy water, Pixie. But next time, be more gentle."*

Link waggled his wings, and silver pixie dust trailed out from one wing. "Couldn't have Kara weeping and wailing all night had you died."

I sighed. "Now what?"

Link pointed into the distance. "I think there might be some caves over by the mountains."

I hitched the backpack higher onto my back and nodded. "Let's get going. We need to find something before the snow *really* starts falling."

The three of us quickly and quietly made our way across the icy lake and onto the snow-packed road. We could follow the two-lane path back into town, or continue straight and hopefully find shelter in the caves.

We went straight and hoped to find a cave.

For fifteen minutes, I wrestled with whether or not we'd made the right decision. We were almost to the mountain, but as exhaustion and fatigue settled in, I could feel my strength draining away. I wasn't sure how much longer I could go on. I was about to voice my fears when Link broke the silence.

"I think I see something in the ridge up ahead," Link said. "Let me fly closer and see."

As he zipped away, Savage snapped his head in my direction and glared. *"My paws are feeling chaffed. All this ice is burning my pads."*

"Would you like me to carry you?"

"I don't want to appear weak, but it may come to that." He

flicked his tail at me. *"And just so you know, you will have to ply me with dozens of treats before I forget this little adventure."*

I laughed. "Deal."

Link zipped back over to us, excitement lighting his eyes. "I found a cave. It's cold but dry."

"Music to my ears," I said. "Lead the way."

19

The interior of the cave was indeed cold and dark, yet it was the howling wind that truly made it feel haunting. Whispering the spell I'd learned from the twins, I conjured up a light orb to illuminate the inside of the cavern. An ethereal light reflected off the shimmering blue walls and stalactite and stalagmite icicles.

"This will be a lovely place to die," Savage said as he shook off the snow from his bedazzled coat.

"You aren't going to die," I said. "I'm going to start a fire, and you'll be fine."

"Just promise me if I do *die*, that you'll take me out of this ridiculous coat."

"No promises," Link said.

I set the backpack on the ground and sighed. "At least we have plenty of food and coffee."

"*For a day,*" Savage said. "*What then? We starve to death?*"

I rolled my eyes. "It won't come to that. A lot of people knew where we were going today. Someone will come looking for us tomorrow morning."

Savage glared at me. *"Yes, a lot of people* did *know where we were going today. And one of them nearly killed me!"*

I glanced at Link. "Did you see who attacked us?"

"I'm sorry, lass. I dinna see anyone."

"We'll figure it out." I rubbed my hands over my jacket. "Let's try to find something to burn, and then we can see about food and who might have wanted us dead."

"Do you think that's wise, Kara?" Link asked. "Lighting a fire, I mean. The warmth of the fire could cause our surrounding area to become unstable."

"If we want to survive the night," I said, "I don't think we'll have a choice."

"My paws could use some heat," Savage admitted.

"Then it's settled," Link said. "We go hunting for firewood."

I looked around the stark, icy cave. "I don't think we'll find any wood in here."

Link shook his head. "Nope. But I spotted a giant pine tree near here. I can gather some pine needles and pinecones."

"I'll go with you," I said.

"No, Kara. You stay here. Empty the backpack, and I'll take that with me."

I quickly dumped out the contents of the backpack—thermos half filled with coffee, another thermos half filled with chicken noodle soup, one muffin, and two cookies. "I almost forgot." I unzipped my coat pocket and withdrew two protein bars. "This is a lot of food. We'll be okay until help comes."

Savage looked up from grooming one paw. *"Are you trying to convince yourself, or me?"*

Link swooped down and pick up the empty backpack before

zipping out the cave's entrance, his laughter bouncing off the frozen walls.

I spent the next few minutes doing my best to clear a space for the fire and a place for us to hunker down and sleep for the night. I'd just finished, with zero help from Savage, when Link flittered inside the cavern. From the look on his face, I could tell the backpack was heavy, and that Link was freezing cold.

"This should keep us warm," Link said as he dangled the backpack near my face.

Reaching out, I grabbed the bag and dumped half the pinecones onto the ground, being careful to make sure none of them rolled away. Once they were in a makeshift pyramid atop some pine needles, I whispered a fire spell and grinned as the pinecones sparked, and then burned.

Link and Savage both wasted no time and hunkered down close to the fire.

"Believe it or not," I said, "the soup and coffee are still warm. I'll just set out everything, and we can have a nice meal close by the fire."

"I've been thinking about who could have attacked us," Link said as he nibbled on a cookie. "If we take Lila at her word, and she was at the house yesterday, then I think we can eliminate her as a suspect. But we have to look at her husband. Plus, we just came from their house."

I took a sip of the coffee and nodded. "That's true. But can Bruno do magic?"

"We'll need to find out," Link said.

"Jessica Weston and Brody Billings both knew where we were going," I said. "And they both can wield magic."

Link nodded. "And if we can prove Zelda was at her shop during the time of the attack, then we can eliminate her as a suspect."

"Good thinking," I said, tossing Savage a piece of chicken from the soup.

"My life has been reduced to begging for scraps," Savage said around a mouth full of chicken. *"What dastardly deed will happen next?"*

No sooner had he spoken the words than a rumble filled the cavern and the ground beneath us shook. Before I could comprehend what was going on, massive clumps of snow filled the cavern entrance, trapping us inside.

"Appears we've just had an avalanche," Link said.

"Why am I not surprised?" Savage mused.

I laughed. "Well, it's sort of your fault, Savage. You had to ask what would happen next."

"An avalanche might be a good thing," Link said. "Maybe it'll help trap heat inside."

"Trap heat? Or trap us?" Savage mused.

I tossed another pinecone onto the fire. "Will this heat be enough for you, Link?"

Link shrugged and leaned back against a thermos. "I figure there will be at least a couple more hours of heat from the thermos."

"And after that?" I asked.

Savage sighed and set the paw he'd been grooming on the ground. *"Fine. The pixie can sleep next to me. My warmth should be enough for him."*

Link and I stared at each other in amazement.

I was the first to recover. "That's kind of you, Savage."

"Don't mention it," he said. *"And I mean it. Don't ever mention it."*

I chuckled. "It'll be our little secret, Savage. What happens in the icy cavern, stays in the icy cavern."

20

I reached behind me to pull the covers over my shivering body. I was freezing. When my hand fell on dirt and not a blanket, I blinked my eyes open in surprise...and stared across at Savage and Link curled up together. I'd have given anything for my phone not to be at the bottom of the frozen lake so I could take a picture. No way would they *ever* admit to the nicety otherwise.

"Good morning, Kara," Link said as he pushed Savage's paw away. "Glad to see we survived the night."

"Fire's still holding on as well." I reached over and tossed two more pinecones onto the dwindling fire. "Now we just have to come up with a plan to get out of here." I glanced around the icy cavern and shuddered. "I wish I knew what time it was. It's freaky being underground like this. I can't tell anything."

Savage yawned loudly, stood, and stretched in the weird way cats do with their front legs out as far as they can go and their butt near the ground. *"Stand back. I got this covered."*

"What do you mean you have this covered?" I demanded as I

took a sip of the cold coffee in the thermos. I could have used magic to heat it, but I didn't have the energy. I was definitely not a girl who did well sleeping on the ground. "What are you going to do?"

Savage grinned. Or at least I assumed that was what he'd attempted to do. *"Watch and see, Valkyrie."*

He sashayed to the entrance of the cave, his tail swishing back and forth as he strutted. I glanced at Link, but he just shrugged. Neither of us had any idea what Savage was going to attempt.

My tuxedo cat stopped in front of the massive mound of snow, stood on his hind legs, lifted his front paws high in the air…and popped out his razor-sharp claws. He reminded me of The Wolverine from the Avengers.

"You two aren't the only ones who can work magic," Savage said. *"Stand back and be prepared to be amazed by Savage. The Cat. The Myth. The Legend."*

And amazed I was.

It was as if he'd bathed in a tub full of catnip. His front claws moved so quickly, I barely registered the movement. He flew back and forth in front of the entrance like a typewriter moving across the page—the snow whipping behind him in a fine mist. When he came to a dense area, he pivoted and used his back legs to kick out a mound of snow.

Just when I was about to call out for him to take a break and rest, the last of the snow gave way, and a beam of light illuminated the cave.

"Would you look at that," Link said. "The little beast did it."

"Extra treats for a month!" I cried.

Savage turned to me and retracted his claws. *"Two."*

I laughed. "Extra treats for *two* months."

"Grab the backpack and let's get back to town," Link said. "I'm ready to get this case solved and get back to civilization."

"Leave the ridiculous jacket behind," Savage said. *"Give it an honorable death."*

I laughed again and tossed the jacket, two empty thermoses, half a muffin, and one power bar into the backpack before slinging it over my shoulder. "We can't leave the jacket. It was given to us. But I agree with Link. I'm ready to get back to my cottage and leave all this snow and ice behind me."

I knocked down the last of the snow and stepped out into the blinding world. The combination of dark cave and glaring sun on fresh snow gave me an instant headache.

"Of all the times not to have sunglasses," I grumbled.

"Or a phone," Link said. "But at least it's not snowing right now."

We'd been trudging slowly toward town for about fifteen minutes when I heard the faint sound of a snowmobile in the distance. "Look alive, friends. We got company coming."

The snowmobile crested the top of the hill, and I waved my arms in the air, hoping to get their attention. It worked. The snowmobile veered off the course it was on and headed straight for us. When the driver was almost on top of us, Link and I both laughed when we saw who it was.

"I was on my way to save your butts," Rota said as she yanked off her helmet and stood up from the snowmobile. "You all look terrible."

I threw my arms around my grandmother, almost knocking us both to the ground. "I'm so glad to see you!"

"Same here, Granddaughter."

Her arms tightened around me, and I breathed her in.

"Tell me what happened," she demanded as she pushed me away.

I told her about the magical attack, the snowmobile at the bottom of the lake, our sleepover in the cave, and Savage's heroic escape this morning.

"That's quite a story," Rota said.

"How did you know where to look for us?" I asked.

"When you didn't answer your phone last night," Rota said, "I got worried. Then when Zane called around ten to tell me he was getting on the plane to start home from Russia, and he couldn't reach you, he asked me where you were. I had to admit to him I couldn't reach you, either."

I groaned. "He's going to be worried."

"We'll call him in a minute. Anyway, I called PADA immediately after hanging up with Zane last night, and I had them ping your phone. That's when they told me where it was. I had to wait until daylight to take the ship over here to Winter Island. I rented a snowmobile from that Brody guy and hauled butt out here to where your phone disappeared."

"So Brody was working?" I mused. "Interesting. He knew where we were going yesterday."

Rota scowled. "I'll snap his scrawny little neck myself if he attacked you."

Link and I laughed.

"We don't know he's the culprit," I said. "Can I use your phone to call Zane? I don't want him to worry any more than he already is."

"Oh, he's worried all right." Rota handed me her phone. "He's called me every half hour since six this morning."

I pulled up Zane's number and waited impatiently for him to answer.

"I get extra treats for two months," Savage informed Rota.

Rota bent down and scratched his chin. "Thanks for saving my granddaughter."

"Hello," Zane said in my ear. "Is that you, Rota?"

My heart leaped in my chest at the sound of Zane's voice. "Hey! It's me, Kara. I'm okay. You can stop worrying."

"I won't stop worrying until I get my arms around you."

I smiled. "That sounds nice. I'm here with Rota, Link, and Savage, and we're heading back to the B&B now."

"We are somewhere over the Atlantic Ocean, and still four hours from PADA headquarters. I have someone meeting me at the airport to transport the fugitive for me so PADA can fly me home immediately."

"You don't have to do that, Zane," I said. "We're okay now. You can see your assignment through to the end."

Zane growled low in my ear. "I just spent two hours on a conference call with the higher-ups at PADA. This is getting out of hand. We need a division within PADA that does nothing but remote apprehension. I found this Yeti north of the arctic circle. That's almost two thousand miles northeast of Moscow." He sighed. "Let's hope PADA gets a plan of action going soon."

"I agree. And again, you don't have to come straight home. You can drop off your prisoner."

"I'm coming home to you, Kara."

I shivered at his seductive tone. "Sounds good. You'll have to come to Winter Island, I'm sure. We may not be finished with our investigation by tonight. Hopefully we will, but maybe not."

"I'll find you, Kara."

"Bye, Zane."

"Stay safe, my love."

I disconnected and handed the phone back to Rota. She grunted and shoved it inside her coat pocket.

"I'm freezing," she said. "Hop on and let's get back to the B&B. Gwendolyn is worried about you as well."

"Where are we all going to sit?" Savage demanded.

"We'll all fit," I said. "Don't worry, Savage."

"Kara can sit behind me and hold on," Rota said. "Savage, you can sit in front of me while Link travels in someone's pocket."

"Sounds good to me." I plopped down on the back end of the snowmobile. "I can't wait to take a nice, warm shower."

21

"Are you sure you've gotten enough to eat?" Gwendolyn asked for the third time as she flittered around the kitchen table.

I patted my swollen belly. "I'm so full, I probably won't be able to walk up the stairs for another fifteen minutes."

"I feel the same way." Link reached across the table and snatched up a cookie. "Well, maybe I can be persuaded to eat just one more."

"I just feel *awful* about what happened." Gwendolyn picked up the empty soup tureen off the table. "Are you warm enough? Should I turn up the heat?"

"We're fine," I told her. "I promise."

Gwendolyn sighed, set the empty soup tureen back on the table, and dropped down into a chair. "I was so scared. I barely slept a wink the entire night. Just thinking about the three of you out there in the cold, maybe lost, maybe hurt." She ran her hands over her face. "First Mya, and then you three."

"I'm sorry we worried you," I said.

"You worried me as well," Rota grumbled as she shoved the last of her grilled cheese sandwich into her mouth. "I paced so much, Alfred was sure he would need to replace the flooring."

I leaned over and rested my hand on Rota's arm. "I'm sorry for scaring you."

Rota patted my hand. "I know you are. Now, let's get upstairs and get some work done. We need to get this case solved."

Over our loud protests, Gwendolyn insisted we take a tray of hot tea and cookies up to our room. Rota was staying in the room next to me. We parted ways at our doors, with Rota promising she'd be right over as soon as she grabbed something from her room.

I shut the door with my foot and carried the tray over to the desk.

"Is any of that for me?" Savage asked.

"You want a cookie?"

"I wouldn't say no." He jumped down off the bed and strolled over to where I stood. *"I hope it's an oatmeal-raisin cookie."*

"You're in luck," I said, placing the cookie on a napkin and setting it on the floor. "One oatmeal-raisin cookie."

My bedroom door opened, and Rota strode in carrying a gift bag and the seax knife she'd given me a couple months ago. The seax had originally belonged to my great-great-great-many-more-greats grandmother. What made it even more powerful was the fact Bettina and Zahara had warded the seax for protection. And trust me, it worked beautifully. After warding the seax, the twins had thrown some powerful magic at me, and I could fend it off with just the seax.

"In case you need it," Rota said, handing me the knife.

"More than once I've kicked myself for not having it," I admitted, cradling the sheathed knife lovingly. "But I wasn't on the job when visiting the twins, and so I didn't think to grab it before I left my cottage."

"Alfred went and got it for you," Rota said. "And your Binder."

A Binder was a magical device PADA detectives used to ensnare supernaturals in a bubble and strip them of their powers.

"I'll have to thank him when I get home." I laughed and set the seax on the desk. "Wanna hear something crazy? I fell asleep in the cave to the image of us all sitting around the table eating warmed peanut butter cake and drinking peanut butter bourbon."

"Which brings me to my second gift." Rota handed me the gift bag. "From Alfred."

I peered inside and squealed. "Oh, he's getting a *huge* hug from me when we get home."

Inside was a large piece of peanut butter cake with what I knew would be peanut butter whiskey icing. "What's in the travel mug?"

Rota laughed. "Find out for yourself."

I reached inside the bag and lifted out the cylindrical glass, set the bag on the desk, flipped open the lip of the cup, and sniffed. "Oh, Rota. You make sure you keep hold of that royal fairy real tight. I might try to snag him away."

Rota threw back her head and cackled as I took a sip of the peanut butter whiskey.

"There's a piece of fairy toast in there for Link," Rota said.

Link's wings buzzed excitedly and glowed silver and green. "Bless that old fairy for not forgetting about his friends."

"You want it now?" I asked.

Link shook his head. "I'll eat it before we head back out again tonight in the cold and snow."

"You have somewhere to be later?" Rota asked.

I nodded. "It's Saturday night. On the first Saturday of every month, the townspeople get together in the park and have a winter run. It's mostly different shifters running and witches and fairies selling a few homemade crafts. But the stores will also stay open late. It seems like a large island event. I expect all our suspects, except for one, will probably show."

"Which suspect won't show?" Rota asked.

I snorted. "Well, I initially thought it would be Lila, but now I'm leaning toward her husband, the Yeti shifter. They're over an hour's drive from town, so I doubt they come in." I sat down on the edge of my bed. "I thought maybe Bruno—that's Lila's husband—shifted after we left his place yesterday and just waited for us to cross the lake. But I'm not sure if he can wield magic or not, and I have no idea how fast Yetis can run. Could he have cut across the mountain and beat us to the lake?"

"It's possible," Rota said.

I nodded. "I figured. But I still think it makes more sense for one of the town suspects to have waited for us."

"And don't forget, we still need to talk to Zelda at the apothecary," Link said. "If she was at her shop during the time we were attacked, then that gets her off the hook."

"Same for Brody," I said, suddenly getting excited. "That would mean Jessica is the killer."

Rota clapped her hands together. "And these three suspects will be at the winter run tonight?"

I nodded. "Yes, I believe so."

Rota grinned. "Then we should have our killer soon."

There was a knock on my door, and I rose to answer. Mrs. Fedderman stood there, smiling at me. Before I could say anything, she reached out and hugged me.

"Oh, thank goodness! We've all been so worried. My husband and I are heading home later today, and I just wanted to come see for myself you were alive and well."

I smiled. "Link, Savage, and I are all okay."

"Good. When I got home last night from town and you weren't here, I was worried. Then we had dinner, and you still weren't home." Her chin trembled. "And then the blizzard came, and I was nearly beside myself with worry for you, dear." She placed a hand on her chest. "I had my husband run to my room twice to bring me the calming essential oils I'd purchased earlier from the apothecary. That lovely woman who owns the store helped me find soaps, and lotions, and candles, and even some calming oils." She leaned in. "It didn't help. I still worried."

"You went to the apothecary yesterday?" I mused. "About what time?"

"Oh, I don't know. Let me think." She looked up at the ceiling. "It was probably around three. Latimer and I had afternoon tea at Tabitha's Tea Shoppe again around two. After eating the most delicious petit fours and scones, we walked around a bit and did some shopping."

That meant Zelda was more than likely at the apothecary at the time we were being attacked out on the lake. So I could eliminate Zelda.

"Well," Mrs. Fedderman said, "I won't keep you. I just wanted to make sure you were okay and to say goodbye."

I gave her a quick hug. "Thanks for checking on me. It was lovely meeting you and your husband."

I shut the door and turned back to Link, Rota, and Savage. "You know what that means?"

Link grinned. "Aye, lass. Our killer is likely either Brody Billings or Jessica Weston."

22

"Quite the turnout," Rota said as she tied her scarf tighter around her neck.

"Are you sure you're warm enough?" I asked.

Rota had insisted on wearing thermals and two layers of clothes versus the bulky jacket she'd originally been wearing when she rescued me earlier in the day. She claimed it was hard to move around in and fight. I asked her if she was planning on fighting someone, and she'd grinned and said the night was young and anything could happen.

"I'm fine," Rota snapped. "Don't you worry about me. You focus on finding our two main suspects."

"I'll look from above," Link said before shooting up into the cold, snowy sky.

Savage had insisted on staying at the B&B, which was fine by me. He'd more than earned the salmon and tuna dinner Gwendolyn had prepared for him. When I'd left my room, he was curled up near the fireplace, warming himself.

"Have you heard from Zane?" Rota asked as we surveyed the

dozens of supernaturals milling about, waiting for the race to start.

I shook my head. "Not since he was flying over Missouri." I glanced at my watch. "By my calculations, he should arrive in Mystic Cove within the hour. I assume he'll come straight here from the airport."

"Attention Winter Island supernaturals!" a voice blared over the sound system in the park. "We will start the race in five minutes. Let's gather round on the south side of the park."

Rota and I followed along with the crowd. I had a few citizens smile at me and wave. But overall, most were steering clear.

Link zipped down and hovered between Rota and me, his breath coming out in quick puffs. "I spotted both Jessica and Brody. It wasn't hard. They're over by that pine tree whispering to each other."

Rota and I both whirled around to see where Link pointed. Sure enough, our two suspects had their heads together. Brody gestured to the alley across the street, and Jessica nodded. Brody had gestured to the alleyway Mya had taken when she was murdered—the alley between the apothecary and the post office. I was about to suggest we go interrogate them when Brody turned and headed across the street, and Jessica wandered in the opposite direction.

"Now what?" Rota asked.

"We split up," I said. "Link, you and Rota go—"

"I go with you, Kara," Link said. "Rota has over sixty years' experience with catching bad guys. I know you were a detective in the human world, but the supernatural world is different. I stay with you."

It was on the tip of my tongue to argue…but I knew it would just be my ego talking and not my brain. I nodded once. "Fine. Link and I will take Brody. Rota, you follow Jessica. Be careful."

Rota winked at me. "Same to you, Granddaughter. You got your seax?"

I patted my hip. "I got it and the Binder."

We parted ways, and I jogged through the park and across the street, careful to miss the ice patches in the road. Link stayed with me, but I could tell all these bitterly cold days were taking their toll on him. I stepped up onto the sidewalk and glanced inside the apothécary. Zelda Yarnell was ringing up a customer.

"Why do you think he's returning to the scene of the crime?" I mused as I continued down the side alley. "Is he looking for something?"

"No idea."

I turned the corner to the back side of the buildings...and bumped into Brody.

"What are *you* doing here?" he hissed.

"I could ask you the same thing," I said, pointing to the crime scene tape that was less than twelve feet away. "You shouldn't be back here."

"Haven't you done enough?" Brody demanded. "It's bad enough you drove one of my snowmobiles into the lake, but now you're hounding me."

He tried to look around me, but I blocked his way. "What are you doing back here?"

Brody sighed and glared down at me. "I'm waiting for someone, if you must know."

A loud bang sounded behind me, and a cheerful cry filled the air. The race had started.

I frowned. "Waiting for someone? Who?"

Link whipped out his sword and waved it in the air. "And ye better not lie to us, or I'll give ye a skelpit lug!"

I let out a bark of laughter. "What?"

Link grinned and twirled his sword. "Basically means I'll give him a slap on the ear."

"You two are insane," Brody said. "Now, can you just go, please? I'm expecting someone."

"Who?" I demanded.

Brody scowled. "None of your business."

I planted my fists on my hips and scowled back. "Care to rephrase that?"

Brody rolled his eyes and sighed. "I'm waiting for Karina Talbott, if you must know."

"And who is she?" I asked.

"She's a customer of Jessica's. I've had my eye on her for a few weeks now, and Jessica told me the other night when I spoke with her on the phone that Karina was asking about me." He wiped his gloved hands on his pants. "She wanted to meet up with me tonight and talk."

"And you chose this location?" I mused. "Why?"

Brody shook his head. "I didn't set up the meeting. Jessica did. She called me this morning and said she spoke with Karina again and Karina said she'd meet me behind the post office at six." He looked at his watch. "Which is now." He made a shooing motion with his hands. "So you gotta leave."

"Crap!" I looked at Link. "It's Jessica! She purposely split us up."

"Let's go!" Link cried.

I whirled and sprinted back down the side alley, nearly slipping on a patch of ice. When I reached the sidewalk, I scanned the area, looking for a glimpse of Rota.

"Do we know where she went?" I asked.

"She went in the opposite direction," Link said. "But there are two choices. I'll take to the sky again. You go across the street and to the left, and I'll go straight."

screamed, her wild mess of hair looking even wilder as it whipped frantically around her head. "Look at you. Beautiful. Dating the fallen angel. You don't know what it's like to have people talk about you. Treat you like you're inferior." She threw three more ice daggers my way. "I knew if Mya told people I had a skin disorder because of the mushrooms, my business would be ruined! I would be financially bankrupt!"

I effortlessly batted the ice shards aside. I was almost in front of Jessica, which meant I had three choices—I could throw out my Binder and hope she didn't cut me with her ice shards before I could throw the magical detainer. I could put my seax away and fight her using magic. Or I could engage her in hand-to-hand combat.

My vote was hand-to-hand combat.

"I was an orphan," I said. "I never knew I had family until six months ago. Don't assume you know anything about me, Jessica."

"Then you should understand where I'm coming from!"

We stood in front of each other, both of us panting. Each of us waiting for the other to strike. The minute she lifted her hands, I leaned back and landed a roundhouse kick to her upper body. Shockingly, Jessica staggered backward, but didn't fall. Usually, when I used my supernatural strength, my opponents would sail through the air. Not so with Jessica. I'd barely gotten my foot on the ground before she let out a guttural scream and charged me.

Much to my delight.

It was going to be a street brawl!

My favorite!

The impact of her head plowing into my chest caused me to sail backward as her arms engulfed me...my back and head hitting the exterior of the building. Lifting my arms, I slammed them down over her head and shoulders, and Jessica cried out in pain and she scrambled out of my reach.

As I propelled myself off the building's edge, adrenaline coursed through me. I swiftly raised my right fist and delivered two sharp jabs to her face. Jessica let out a piercing scream and doubled over, blood streaming from her nose.

I was about to finish her off…when Zane landed next to me, his wings blocking my view of Jessica. Dressed in a black Armani suit, tailored wool jacket, and snow dotting his hair and clothes, he looked breathtakingly gorgeous and totally out of place in our back-alley brawl.

"Allow me, Kara." He whipped out his Binder and encased Jessica in a magical bubble that immediately stripped her of all magical powers.

"I had her," I panted.

"I could see that."

"You came straight here?" I asked.

"Barbie called as I landed in Mystic Cove. She knew about the evidence found at the crime scene and came in to the lab to run the traces found on the victim's jacket. They were mushroom spores."

I laughed. "Too bad she was still on vacation yesterday. That information would have come in handy then."

I turned to look at Rota. She was still on the ground, but Zelda and Link were next to her. I grabbed Zane's hand and together we ran to Rota's side.

"I hope you don't mind that I took down your shield," Zelda said. "But I couldn't apply the poultice otherwise."

"It's fine." I knelt down next to Rota's head. "How are you?"

"Some pain," she whispered. "It'll pass."

"These are deep cuts," Zelda said. "I've been able to stop a lot of the bleeding, but she needs more than what I can do."

"Sheriff Stiles should be here shortly," Zane said. "I called him from the airport. He was out on a call, or I'd have flown him over with me. He had to take the pirate ship, so he's probably thirty to forty minutes out still."

"I'll stay here with Jessica until Sheriff Stiles gets here to take her away," I said. "Fly Rota to Alfred. He'll know what to do. Between Alfred and the twins, Rota will be good as new in no time."

Zane leaned over and kissed me hard on the lips, then gently gathered Rota in his arms.

"Link, you staying here or going with Zane?" I asked.

Link looked back and forth from Rota to me.

"I'll stay with you, Kara," Link said, blue pixie dust leaking from one wing. "You and me. We see this through to the end."

Zane nodded once, unfurled his wings, and took to the snowy sky.

23

"Are you sure you're feeling okay, Rota?" I asked as I handed my grandmother a bourbon.

Rota snorted and raised her glass in the air. "You mean, should I be drinking this?"

I nodded. "Okay. Should you be drinking that?"

It had only been two days since Rota had been slashed with three deadly ice shards. Two had pierced her skin, leaving deep grooves on her body, but the other one had just been a superficial wound and only required stitches.

Zane had called Crystal Nobel when he arrived at his place and told her what had transpired, and Crystal had flown to Winter Island to take Link, Savage, and me back to Zane's mansion. Bettina and Zahara were already at the mansion helping Alfred with potions to heal Rota. My dad, Callum, had even stopped by to see if he could lend a hand with Rota's healing.

But that had been two days ago, and according to Rota at breakfast this morning, she was feeling well enough to have the twins, Crystal, and my dad over for dinner to say thank you for all they'd done for her. That made Zane laugh because we all knew it would be Alfred who prepared the meal.

"One won't hurt her, Kara," my dad said as he sat down on the couch.

"I'm feeling better today than I felt last week," Rota said. "I should undergo extensive repair more often."

Zahara laughed. "Let's not."

Alfred had banished us to the sitting room after dinner so he could clean up and prepare dessert. I was passing out the after-dinner drinks while Zane told the others about his recent apprehension of a Yeti in the Arctic Circle.

"I thought it was cold on Winter Island," Crystal said. "And I was only there long enough to pick up Link and Kara. No way would I want to travel where you were, Zane."

"Hopefully, I won't be traveling that far much longer," Zane said as he sat next to me on the settee. "PADA is taking steps right now to develop a new division within their branches."

"What exactly would they do?" Rota asked.

"The plan is to bring together a full team who will travel to remote locations and solve cases and apprehend supernatural criminals."

"A full team?" I mused.

Zane took a sip of his whiskey. "A forensic scientist with a traveling lab, two detectives, and a team leader to make sure everything is in order."

"You think it will happen?" Bettina asked.

Zane smiled. "There's already been whispers about who might take on such a role."

"Well, I for one am glad," I said. "It will keep you from traipsing off to obscure locations."

Alfred stepped inside the sitting room pushing a wheeled cart piled high with decadent desserts. There was a mixed-berry cheesecake, oatmeal-raisin cookies, lemon bars, and a peanut butter cake with peanut butter whiskey icing.

I jumped up from the couch when he rolled to a stop in the room. "Let me help you, Alfred."

Link laughed. "You just want the first piece of cake."

"Rota told me Savage has developed a taste for oatmeal-raisin cookies," Alfred said. "I have two cookies set aside in the kitchen for you to take home tonight, Kara."

"That's so thoughtful, Alfred," I said. "Thank you."

I took everyone's order and passed out the desserts. We all laughed and chatted as we scarfed down the amazing desserts Alfred had baked. We were just finishing up when Zane's cell phone rang.

"It's PADA," he said, standing to walk out of the room.

"Wonder what that's about?" Zahara mused. "Surely you guys don't have another case already. You just closed this one a couple days ago."

We didn't have long to wait before Zane returned, looking grim.

"Well?" I asked.

Zane shook his head. "You aren't going to believe this one."

"What?" Rota and I both demanded.

"It seems there's a supernatural assisted living facility that is needing PADA's help."

I frowned. "How do they expect us to help?"

Zane grinned and downed the last of his whiskey. "They want us to go undercover. Rota is to pose as a new resident. I'm the concerned grandson, and you are a volunteer staff member."

Rota clapped her hands together. "Sounds like fun!"

"Sounds insane," I said.

"When do we leave?" Rota demanded, downing the last of her drink. "I can be ready in half an hour."

Zane laughed. "We'll leave first thing in the morning."

* * *

Are you ready for the next book in the Kara Hilder series, *Assisted Murder*? Then click here to find out what happens when Zane, Kara, and Rota go undercover at a supernatural assisted living facility. My Book

* * *

Join Jenna's Newsletter: https://jennastjamesbooks.com/newsletter

Other Series by Jenna St. James

Looking for a paranormal cozy series about a midlife witch looking to make a new start with a new career? Then A Witch in the Woods is the book series for you! A game warden witch, a talking/flying porcupine, and a gargoyle sheriff! Check out Book 1, *Deadly Claws:* My Book

. . .

Do you love the idea of a time-traveling, cold-case solving witch? Then Lexi and her side-kick detective familiar, Rex the Rat, are just what you're looking for! Check out their first stop to 1988 in *Time After Time* My Book

Have you read the hilarious adventures of Ryli Sinclair and Aunt Shirley? This traditional cozy mystery series is always fast-paced and laugh-out-loud funny. But what else would you expect from Aunt Shirley—a woman who has at least two deadly weapons on her at all times and carries her tequila in a flask shoved down her shirt? Book 1 is *Picture Perfect Murder*! My Book

Love the idea of a bookstore/bar set in the picturesque wine country of Sonoma County? Then join Jaycee, Jax, Gramps, Tillie, and the whole gang in this traditional cozy series as they solve murders while slinging suds and chasing bad guys in this family-oriented series. First book is *Murder on the Vine!* My Book

Or maybe you're in the mood for a romantic comedy…heavy on comedy and light on sweet romance? Then the Trinity Falls series is for you! My Book

. . .

Love the idea of a Valkyrie witch teaming up with a Fallen Angel to solve crimes? Then the paranormal cozy series, A Kara Hilder Mystery, should be right up your alley! This crime-solving duo not only works for their supernatural town of Mystic Cove, but they also work for the Paranormal Apprehension and Detention Agency—which means they travel a lot to take down bad guys. Find out what happens when a Valkyrie with magical abilities teams up with a Fallen Angel in Book 1, *Sounds of Murder* My Book

ABOUT THE AUTHOR

Jenna writes in the genres of cozy/paranormal cozy/ romantic comedy. Her humorous characters and stories revolve around over-the-top family members, creative murders, and there's always a positive element of the military in her stories. Jenna currently lives in Missouri with her fiancé, step-daughter, Nova Scotia duck tolling retriever dog, Brownie, and her tuxedo-cat, Whiskey. She is a former court reporter turned educator turned full-time writer. She has a Master's degree in Special Education, and an Education Specialist degree in Curriculum and Instruction. She also spent twelve years in full-time ministry.

When she's not writing, Jenna likes to attend beer and wine tastings, go antiquing, visit craft festivals, and spend time with her family and friends. Check out her website at http://www.jennastjames.com/. Don't forget to sign up for the newsletter so you can keep up with the latest releases! You can also friend request her on Facebook at jennastjamesauthor/ or catch her on Instagram at authorjennastjames.

Made in the USA
Columbia, SC
24 September 2023